The Yankee Star
A Collection of
Two Rivers Station
Short Westerns

Robert Peecher

For information the author may be contacted at

PO Box 967; Watkinsville GA; 30677

or at robertpeecher.com

This is a work of fiction. Any similarities to actual events in whole or in part are purely accidental. None of the characters or events depicted in this novel are intended to represent actual people.

For Jean

CONTENTS

THE YANKEE STAR

"You should have drawed down, boy."

Deputy U.S. Marshal Jack Bell lifted his hat from his head, and it was like someone turned a bucket upside down on him. Bell wiped his forehead of the sweat, but it still stung in his eyes. It didn't help, neither, that his face was covered in dust so that the sweat just dragged silt down into his eyes.

But Bell didn't worry about the dust and sweat in his eyes. He kept his eyes open and on the black man in the cavalry uniform standing in front of him. Faced with the Henry rifle pointing death at him, the man had dropped his six shooter onto the sandy dirt.

"You would have shot me dead if I did," the black man said.

"Yep," Bell answered. "But being killed would have been a damn sight better than having to walk out of this desert."

Bell slid down out of his saddle and took the lead

1

rope in one hand while keeping the Henry rifle trained on the fugitive. "Take a step back away from that six shooter. I'm going to mosey on over and pick it up. If you move for the gun, or you move for me, you won't have any walking to do."

The fugitive chuckled in spite of his predicament. "Is that a warning or an offer?"

"Yep," Bell said. "Now step back."

The man took a couple of steps away from the belt and holstered gun on the ground.

"Why don't you just shoot me if you want to shoot me?" the man said.

"This Yankee star on my chest says I can't shoot you unless you give me cause. But it doesn't say I have to share my water with you, so I hope for your sake that canteen over your shoulder is plenty full."

Bell stowed the six shooter in his saddle bag. He pointed with the Henry rifle back toward the east, the way they'd come. "Start walking."

Bell had driven his horse pretty hard out across this brutal hot desert, so with his fugitive on foot, Bell decided to walk a bit to give Petey a break. He couldn't guess how far they'd come into the west Texas desert, but he knew they wouldn't see water for a couple of days. At least not at a walking pace.

"You could leave me out here," the fugitive said. "I'll probably die anyway."

"It ain't my job to leave you," Bell said. "You kill a U.S. Army corporal at a U.S. Army fort and steal a horse that's the property of the United States government, and it's my job to bring you in."

"You a Confederate?" the black man asked. "You sound like a Confederate."

"I was," Bell said.

"Give you pleasure to take a colored man into custody?"

"Taking a man into custody don't make me feel one way or the other," Bell said. "It's just what they pay me to do."

"I warn't no slave. I was born free up north."

"That ain't none of my concern, neither," Bell said.

***

They walked on in silence for a while through the harsh landscape, rocky and dusty without much vegetation. And what grass there was, it was all brown. The low trees looked like dead sticks shoved into the ground. And the sun beat down unmercifully. The occasional tree or stump of a hill served as the only landmarks on this flat, open terrain, and a slow progress made it hard to distinguish any progress at all.

Bell fought the urge to have a drink of water. He had plenty to last him and his horse Petey, the cavalry gelding he'd stolen at the end of the war. Deputy Marshal Bell had filled up three canteens before riding out from Jacksboro. He'd chased this boy for three days out from Jacksboro. Bell had not before traveled this far west. He knew that somewhere ahead of them was the Llano Estacado – the great Staked Plain, a tableland that was refuge for the Comanche and the Kiowa – and at its base the White River.

Bell's fear had been that his fugitive would reach the river, gain water, and then disappear up into the Llano Estacado. He'd never been so far west as to have seen it, but Bell had heard stories that made him fear traveling into this wasteland.

The first day and a half, he tracked the fugitive along the Brazos River, and water was not a concern. But then the trail ventured away from the river, out into the dusty plain, and water was scarce.

On the third day he came across the carcass of the stolen U.S. cavalry horse, and Jack Bell knew he'd get his man before he could reach the Staked Plain.

"What happened to the horse?" Bell asked, though he already knew the answer.

"Stumbled in a prairie dog hole and threw me. He broke a leg, and there wasn't nothing I could do but shoot him."

"Damn shame," Bell said.

"It don't matter. They'll hang me whether I bring the horse back or not."

"That's not what I meant," Bell said.

"What'd you mean, then?"

Bell spit dust. "If you hadn't had to shoot that horse, we could ride out of here and be back a damn sight sooner."

"Getting home fast is more important to you than a man's life?"

"You've put me to some trouble," Bell said. "Whatever happens to you now is your own doing. None of that is any reason for me not to want to be home."

Bell lifted his hat and swept his sleeve across his forehead again. The sun was pounding on him, and he'd have paid good money at that moment for a spot in the shade and some of his wife's sweet tea.

The warrant in Jack Bell's saddlebag said that the man's name was Clifton Webber and that he was wanted for murder and horse theft. Bell knew a bit more than that. When the U.S. Judge, Fitzsimmons, handed him the warrant, he told Bell some of the particulars. Clifton Webber was a cavalry soldier, what they would soon call a Buffalo Soldier, though no one had yet heard that term. A colored man serving in the 9th Cavalry, Clifton Webber had been at Camp Wichita, an intermediate station between Fort Richardson, which was down near Jacksboro, and Two Rivers Station, the place Jack Bell called home. The camp existed to protect frontier settlements from the kinds of raids by Comanches that had killed Bell's parents and brothers, the kind of raid Bell himself had fought off just a couple of years before.

"Ain't you want to know why I killed that man and took that horse?" Clifton Webber asked.

"Not particularly," Bell said. "Ain't my business to know why you done it."

What Bell knew was that Webber had killed a corporal at Camp Wichita and fled the camp on a cavalry horse. Webber had fled south at first, going toward Jacksboro, and then he'd struck out west across the plains. A day after the murder, word reached Fitzsimmons, the federal judge in Sherman. Bell happened to be in Sherman that same day, and Fitzsimmons handed Bell the warrant.

"Go and find him and bring him in," Fitzsimmons instructed. "He'll be court martialed in the army court, so it's not really my case. But the 9th Cavalry can't be riding all over Texas hunting a fugitive when its place is protecting homesteads. So you go and bring him in."

Bell sent word home to Two Rivers Station to let his wife know he'd be away a bit longer, and then he immediately started south to Jacksboro to try to pick up the trail.

"You're taking me back so they can hang me. Least you can do is know why I done what they hanging me for."

"Whether or not they hang you ain't my business," Jack Bell said. "Maybe the military court will listen to your reasoning. Maybe they won't. But none of that matters none to me. They sent me out to track you down and bring you back. That's what I'm doing."

The sun was inescapable and the heat was almost more than he could bear. Clifton Webber lifted the canteen that was strapped over his shoulder and gave it a shake. There was not much water left.

"I got to stop," he said. "I got to have a drink."

Bell took off his hat and poured some water into it. The Stetson Plains hat was so tight it could be used as a bucket to hold water. Bell held the hat to Petey's muzzle and let the horse drink from it. Bell took a drink from his canteen.

"I ain't going to have enough water to make it," Webber said.

Bell took hold of Webber's canteen and shook it. The thing was near dry.

"A man planning on making a run across the dry plains ought to fill his canteen," Bell said.

"I was makin' a run, so I was in a hurry," Webber said, and chuckled at his joke. "Yes sir, I was in a hurry."

Jack Bell, and all the other frontier settlers, depended on the cavalry. The presence of the army meant that Bell and other settlers had less to fear from Comanche raids. The presence of the army meant that Bell had some confidence when he was away from home that the Comanche warriors would not stray so near to Two Rivers Station. As such, Bell didn't have any patience for a man who would desert. Chasing Webber out across the dry plains, he'd conjured Webber up as a vile criminal. But now, face to face with the man, he couldn't help but like Webber, at least a little bit. Clifton Webber was a convivial sort, smiling and chuckling though Bell's appearance surely meant Webber would soon face a rope.

"How much water you got?" Webber asked.

"Enough for me and my horse," Bell said. "If there's any left, I'll share. But you'd better make the most of what you've got. Now, get back to walking."

They walked on a little ways, but not far, when Webber started talking again.

"I didn't sign up for the army to kill women and children," Webber said.

"I suspect not."

"We was riding patrol. They'd been an attack on a ranch a few days before, and we left out of Camp Witchita to see if we could find a trail. Coming up on dusk, we found a Comanche camp. Snuck up on it from behind a hill. We could see they was women and children in the camp, but they was men, too. We figured that was the party that made the raid on the ranch. We didn't wait. We didn't scout them to see what we was really dealing with. The captain ordered a charge, and we charged."

Hearing him talk about it, Jack Bell thought involuntarily of Brandy Station. He'd been there with JEB Stuart, a lieutenant in the Confederate cavalry. Bell knew what it meant to ride in a cavalry charge. He knew what kind of carnage a cavalry charge could commit.

"But the men we seen was old men, they wasn't warriors at all. If the warriors that made that raid on the ranch was with this camp, they wasn't there when we rode down on them. But that didn't stop us. Women and children," Webber said, and his voice broke. "We killed women and children."

Bell was walking behind Webber where he could keep his eyes on his prisoner. He watched as Webber reached a hand up to his face to brush away the dust that he gotten in his eye.

Clifton Webber was a big man, powerfully built. An imposing figure. Bell kept enough distance between them that if Webber decided to turn and come at him, Bell would have time to drop him with the Colt revolver on his hip. But even a big man can be haunted by ghosts, Bell thought.

"I seen their faces," Webber said. "I seen their faces in my mind when I closed my eyes. The first one I came to was an old man. He had a spear and was standing his ground. I cut him down. I didn't even know he was an old man until I'd already swung the saber, and I saw him, clear as I'm looking at them hills yonder, I saw him. He was yelling and had that spear, and I swung my saber, and as it cut into his chest, I saw his face. And I thought he was too old, but I rode on. I rode on into the camp with my saber above my head. They was a woman, she had something in her arms, and she was running. I rode down on her and swung my saber, and she looked up at me as I swung it. And I realized she had a baby in her arms."

Webber shook his head.

"I pulled my horse up and rode off out of the camp. I couldn't do it no more. I killed an old man and a woman with a baby, and I couldn't do it no more. So I just rode out of the camp and waited. I watched as the others kept going, circling around inside the camp, cutting down old men and women. And children."

Webber walked on a ways farther, the sun beating down on him. When he came to a stop, Bell dropped his hand down to the Colt pistol in his holster and slid the leather thong off of the hammer.

Clifton Webber turned on his heel and looked at the deputy marshal who was bringing him in.

"When it was over, all them boys in the cavalry was congratulating each other, smiling and laughing and talking about what a fine job of Indian fighting we done. But it wasn't no fight. It was slaughter, is what it was. Three days later we was back at camp, and all I could think of was the look on that old man's face, and that woman with the baby in her arms, and I couldn't get them out of my mind. I decided I couldn't do it no more. So I made to leave. I saddled up my horse, and I was leaving Camp Wichita. But the corporal, he seen me and made to stop me."

Bell didn't let go of the Colt. Webber had tears rolling heavy down his face, but Jack Bell figured it was a good chance he'd have to shoot Webber in a minute or two. The man was getting hisself too worked up.

"I told him to back away and let me go," Webber

said. "But he said he'd arrest me for desertion if I didn't stop. But I couldn't stay there. When the corporal made to grab me, I just lost my mind. I didn't even see nothing. I just started punching him. I hit him too much, too hard."

Bell had assumed Webber had killed the corporal with a gun. He did not realize he'd beaten the man to death.

"I ain't saying I don't have sympathy for you," Bell said. "But I'm going to have to insist that you turn around and get to walking."

It was hard to read Clifton Webber. Bell wasn't sure if the man was trying to talk his way out of the hanging rope, convince Bell to turn him loose, or if he was trying to justify his actions. Either way, Jack Bell was paid to bring Clifton Webber back to the fort at Jacksboro. He wasn't being paid to care.

***

"I told you I was born free," Webber said as they marched on through the heat.

"You did."

"I was born up to Ohio. My mama and daddy was both slaves, but they was set free when they master died. They was from Virginia. Worked a tobacco plantation. They moved up to Ohio in a community of free blacks. My daddy had a farm."

"They still there?" Bell asked, not so much from interest.

"They is. I got a whole parcel o' brothers and sisters. I'm the oldest, first one to leave. They was proud when they saw me in my uniform. I'll tell you that. The son o' two freed slaves, they never did think they'd see me in a army uniform. No, sir.

"I growed up helping my daddy on the farm, and I might have been a farmer, too, but when the war was going on I thought I'd like to enlist. I figured if men was fighting and dying to set my people free, I wanted to be right there with them, fighting alongside 'em. Die if I have to. But mama said I couldn't enlist until I was nineteen years old. She made me promise. The war ended in April of '65, and I turned nineteen in August.

"You fought in the war, though, ain't you?"

"I did," Bell said.

"For the Confederacy."

"I did."

"And now here we is, a freed black man from the army being taken to the United States government by a Confederate vet'ran who's wearing a United States badge. Ain't we something?"

"We're a right conundrum," Bell said, not so much in agreement.

"It don't bother you to wear a United States badge after fighting against the United States government?"

"I ain't proud to wear a Yankee badge," Bell said. "But the man who gave me this star is a friend of mine, and I suppose I'm proud to wear it alongside him."

"'A Yankee badge,'" Webber repeated. "Yes, sir. A Yankee badge."

"You don't stop talking much, do you?" Bell said.

The Buffalo Soldier chuckled a hearty, happy laugh.

"Nope, I guess I don't at that. I guess if something's on my mind, I'm bound to say it."

"It ain't becoming," Jack said.

Webber chuckled again. "Well, if I'm bothering you, I suppose I can quit talking. But I'm a man with limited time, and I figure if I gots anything to say, now's the time to say it."

"Hush up," Bell said, and there was a bite to his voice. He wasn't being rude. Jack Bell took two big steps to catch up to Webber and put a hand on his shoulder. "Stop right there and don't say nothing."

Webber looked back and saw Bell's head cocked, saw he was listening for something. And then Webber heard it, too.

They were in a shallow depression with a low hill immediately to their right. On the other side of that hill, both men could hear the noise of people talking in the distance and an occasional horse whinnying.

Petey let out a snort, and Bell patted him on the neck.

"Hate to do this to you, but it's necessary," Bell said. He took out a pair of handcuffs and bound Webber's hands behind his back. Then Bell helped him to sit down on the ground.

"You don't move. I'm going to go up this rise and see what's on the other side."

Bell didn't worry about staking Petey. He wouldn't go anywhere. But he did draw the Henry rifle from the scabbard off Petey's saddle.

Slow and quiet, Bell walked the rise until he neared

the top, and then he crouched down to remain hidden to anything on the other side. As he got up to the crest of the hill, he got down on his hands and knees and scrambled to where he could see over it. Less than a hundred yards down the opposite slope, Bell counted twenty-one Comanche braves. It was a small raiding party.

The braves were loafing about, all of them unhorsed. They weren't going in one direction or another but were stopped to allow the horses to graze, though the grass was meager. Bell figured maybe they were going to eat, or had already eaten. He checked back a few times to make certain Webber wasn't trying to make an escape, but he stayed down on his hands and knees and watched the Comanche for a while to see if he could determine what they were up to.

If they would move on, it wouldn't be a problem to just let the Comanche slide right past, let them go on about their business. It didn't matter much to Bell which direction they went, either, so long as they didn't come up over this hill. But if they'd strike out west, or even head back east, they could be gone before they ever discovered Bell and Webber. But the longer they stayed in this spot, the better the chance they would top this hill.

But the Comanche warriors were unhurried. They neither moved to set up a camp nor mounted up to ride on.

As easy and quiet as he came up the hill, Bell slid back down it.

"Comanche raiding party on the other side of that hill," Bell told Webber. "Not a very big party. A score of them. But more than I care to try to handle on my own."

Webber looked up to the top of the hill.

"What if I let out a great big yell right now?" he said, and his tone was like a rattlesnake bite. "What if I hollered as loud as I could and let them Injuns over that hill know we is here. You'd be bound to ride on lickety-split. Have to leave me here. Maybe I'd rather take my chances with them Injuns than with the army court-martial."

"Don't be a damn fool," Bell said. "Look at what you're wearing, boy. You go to hollering and bring them Injuns over that hill, and you're right. I'll ride off. But what do you think they're going to do when they see you in an army uniform? You think them Comanche will care that you have regrets about being a part of the cavalry that slaughtered women and children? You'll have plenty of opportunity to tell them about it, because they'll kill you slow. They'll kill you for days."

Bell was indifferent. Petey was watered and rested. He didn't have any fear that he would not be able to outrun the Comanche if it came to that. But Clifton Webber would sore regret it if he went to drawing the attention of those Comanche.

"Looks like it don't matter if I go to hollering or not," Webber said, looking at the crest of the hill where Bell had been.

Bell spun on his heel, rifle raised. Standing at the top of the hill were three of the Comanche, ominous outlines against the clear blue sky.

"Damnation," Bell muttered. "Start walking." He gave Webber a shove, and the big cavalryman began to walk, his hands still clasped behind his back.

"You think they're going to let us walk out of here?" Webber said.

"Nope," Bell said. "I think I'm going to have to fight our way out."

***

"They's two of them over your right shoulder," Webber said.

"I'm aware," Bell answered.

The two Comanche warriors had been trailing them for an hour. Private Clifton Webber was talking less and walking faster, and Bell figured they'd probably made three or four miles now. Going was difficult in the heat.

The Comanche had made no effort to hide themselves. They were riding their horses at a slow walk a quarter of a mile to the south of where Bell and Webber walked.

"It ain't the two I can see that I'm nervous about," Bell said.

He'd counted twenty-one Comanche braves, but only two were in sight.

"It'll be dark soon," Webber noted.

"I'm aware," Bell repeated.

"Why you reckon they're just shadowing us like that?" Webber asked.

"They're keeping us from water," Bell said. "The Brazos River is southeast of us. Probably not more than a half day's ride. They're pushing us a little to the northeast, away from the river and away from our best supply of water. Jacksboro is also down that away, and the fort."

"Where's the rest of 'em?" Webber asked. "The ones you's nervous about."

Bell looked out at the horizon to the east where it was already starting to grow shadowy as the sun set in the west.

"I figure they took a big ride, either south or north of us, so that they could find some good ground for an ambush. Out here, you can see forever. There ain't enough hills nor valleys nor bushes for a band of Comanche warriors to hide behind. So they rode on up ahead until they came to a good hill or a dry creek bed, more likely, and they're laying in wait."

"And so we just going to walk into the ambush?"

"I've got to get you back to the fort at Jacksboro," Bell said. "That's what I'm out here to do. The only way I can get you there is to walk in this direction. If there's an ambush up ahead, we'll deal with that when the time comes."

"What about when it gets dark?" Webber asked. "They'll be able to come right up on us."

"I was kind of hoping they'd ambush us before dark," Bell said. "But it don't hardly look now like that's going to happen."

"What'd you say your name is, Marshal?"

"Jack Bell. Deputy United States Marshal Jack Bell."

"You a strange man, Deputy United States Marshal Jack Bell."

"How's that?"

"I ain't never yet heard no man say he was hoping Comanche would attack him before dark."

Clifton Webber laughed his deep laugh, and Bell

found it was infectious. In spite of himself, he cracked a smile. "Nope," Webber said. "Ain't never heard no man hope for a Comanche attack."

They walked on a little ways farther, not more than a mile. In the distance there were hills, but Bell knew they would not reach those hills before dark. The grassland of the plains was now dotted with clumps of sagebrush and clusters of low mesquite trees. Soon, they'd be deep enough in the vegetation that Bell knew the Comanche would be able to stage an ambush. He did not want to get caught there after dark. If the mesquite was thick, and it soon would be, the Comanche would be able to sneak up – bush by bush – until they were right on top of Bell and Webber.

Bell reached out and took hold of Webber's shoulder.

"We're going to stop here," Bell said.

Bell unlatched the handcuffs he'd put on Webber earlier. He didn't like leaving the man in wrist-irons, but he was worried with the appearance of the Comanche that Webber might try something foolish.

"There's a fair amount of sagebrush and mesquite right here," Bell said. "You go and collect some of it so that we can build up a campfire. Don't go no farther than about twenty yards from me. You can get what you need right here. If you go farther than twenty yards, I ain't going to warn you. I'm just going to shoot you. We're in a tight spot right now, and I won't tolerate anything foolish."

Webber rubbed his wrists. "It don't make no difference if you wants to shoot me or the army wants to hang me. Them Injuns is going to kill us before dawn."

The two Comanche who'd been shadowing halted their horses. They were both still mounted, but their horses were just standing. The Comanche were waiting and watching.

"If you don't do like I said, you got more to fear from me than you do them Comanche," Bell said.

Webber collected a couple of armloads of mesquite branches and dropped them at Bell's feet. Bell stood by Petey, rifle in hand, keeping one eye on the two Comanche braves and one eye on Webber.

"More wood," Bell said. "Those dead branches will burn fast. We need enough wood to last us the night."

Webber laughed and shook his head. "We ain't got to worry about lasting the night."

When a sufficient pile of wood was at his feet, Bell put the handcuffs back on Webber, but this time cuffed the wrists to the front so that when dinner was ready, Webber could feed hisself without Bell having to remove the cuffs. He didn't want any chance of Webber trying something as the sun set.

Then Bell got down on his knees and started breaking up the pieces of wood.

"You keep a watch on them two warriors. They do anything other than just sit their horses, you let me know."

He built the fire teepee style with the smallest twigs first, then he ripped up some of the nearby wintergrass and spun it into a loose ball. He struck a match and held it to the wintergrass until it was caught, and then he held the grass down to the smallest of twigs to start the fire. He put on increasingly larger branches until a decent sized fire was going.

Dusk was settled in now, and dark would come along soon. Even so, the Comanche warriors were still well visible, and Bell knew they could see everything he was doing.

Bell casually led Petey around to the north side of the fire, where the fire would burn between the horse and the two Comanche's south of them. He staked Petey's lead to the ground where the horse could get at a few clumps of grass. Bell removed the saddle and brushed the horse down a bit, and he left the saddle off. Petey was staked several feet away from the campfire. Out on the open prairie like this, a man wouldn't typically let his horse be so far away from him. If the Comanche were watching close, they might get suspicious. But Bell doubted they noticed. They were some distance off and it was getting dark.

Bell unrolled his blanket not too far from the campfire and made a big production out of getting all his gear sorted for the night. He laid his saddlebags out by the blanket where he might use them as a pillow and set his saddle down beside it. He took out his cookware – just a tin plate and a small tin pot for coffee. He even unsheathed his Bowie knife and made a big deal out of sticking it in the ground near his bedroll. He did everything he could – more than he would ever typically do – to get ready to bed down for the night.

Webber watched with interest.

Bell poured a little of his water into Webber's canteen and told the man to drink up. He took his tin plate and bacon from his saddlebag and heated it up over the fire. Then he walked over the Petey.

"Come on over here and get you something to eat. Ain't no reason to let the Comanche kill you on an empty stomach."

Webber pushed himself up from the ground where he'd been sitting and walked back toward Bell and the horse. He sat down on the ground there, and Bell put the plate beside him.

Only the faintest bit of light still remained.

Bell climbed up onto Petey's bare back where he had a better vantage, and he scanned the horizon. The fire light nearby made it damn near impossible to see anything in the distance, at least to the south. But he could look around pretty well to the east and north and west. The Comanche who had trailed Bell and Webber were still there, or Bell thought they were. It was so hard to see now that he wasn't sure if he could make them out as shadows against the horizon, or if he was only seeing his last memory of them.

"What you thinking on, Marshal?" Webber asked.

"Just sit still," Bell said. "I don't like our chances against a score of Comanche braves out here on the open plain after dark. If we sit here and wait, we'll be slaughtered. So I'm going to give it a try to see if I can't get us out of this."

Bell got down off Petey's back and walked around a bit, trying to get a better angle to see the Comanche. He walked away from the fire to the west and the south, making a big arc. He walked silently and stood still for a stretch of time to see if he could hear anything.

He even looked back up at the fire to see if its light hit Webber or the horse, but he was satisfied that from a distance the fire did not illuminate his prisoner or Petey.

Now Bell moved quickly.

He walked over to Webber and kneeled down so that they were very close to each other. "I know you're fond of talking," Bell whispered, "but I'm going to have to insist you stay quiet. Don't make a sound, don't talk, no laughing, nothing. Just do what I tell you to do."

Webber nodded his head.

Bell now undid all the work he'd done to get ready to bed down. He did it all quietly and as far away from the fire as he could so that he wasn't lighting himself up or casting shadows. He stowed all his gear — the knife, the plate, the pot, the bedroll. He saddled Petey and quietly, gingerly, replaced the saddlebags.

Bell walked back to the fire and tossed a couple more logs onto it, and then he stacked branches near the fire. Some of the branches he put down in the original fire so that they crossed over into the new stack of branches. Slowly, he hoped, the old fire would burn into the new stack of branches, and it would look from a distance like someone was continuing to feed branches into the fire. Even if the ruse worked only for a couple of hours, that would be all he needed.

Bell looked around. It was all pitch black now. There wasn't much more than a sliver of moon, not enough light to see for any distance.

"You hold those chains on your wrists quiet," Bell whispered to Webber, and then he helped him to his feet. Bell took a bandanna he'd gotten from his saddlebags and wrapped it around the chain of the handcuffs to muffle any noise.

"West," Bell said. "We're walking back the way we come. Silent as a mouse. Start moving."

***

"I ain't sure how much longer I can keep going, marshal," Webber confessed. "I gots to sleep. I'm exhausted."

They'd walked through the night, carving a path straight west and then dropping south. Allowing that they'd gone slow from fatigue, Bell figured they had marched at least fifteen miles in a big, curving arc that took them well around the Comanche warriors. But they probably were still no closer to Jacksboro than they had been at dusk.

For short stretches, Bell had tied a rope around Webber's waist and tied the other end to his pommel and he had ridden in the saddle and dozed some. He wasn't rested, by any stretch, but he could manage a while still. His concern was in making sure he did not become more exhausted than his prisoner. That could be a bad situation and give a desperate man an opportunity for mischief.

Bell was in the saddle now, and until Webber spoke, he'd been riding with his eyes closed. The morning light was up, and Bell now looked out across the horizon in every direction. He saw no sign that the Comanche were still with them.

"They'll be tracking us," Bell said. "At some point in the night, they rushed our camp and only found the fire burning. They realized I tricked them and that we snuck off when they couldn't see us. And they'll be angrier than a hive of hornets, now. How far they are behind us depends entirely on when they rushed the campsite. Were we gone an hour or two or four when they discovered the deception? Even in the dark, they can track us, and now that it's light, they can move faster than we're moving and still follow our trail. If I let you sleep, them Comanche will have me dead before noon."

"Let me rest in your saddle," Webber said. "Please."

Bell sighed heavily. He really didn't want to slide out of the saddle just now. He also wasn't keen on giving Webber an opportunity to give Petey spurs and ride off, though Bell wasn't convinced the horse would run. But the deputy marshal also understood that if Webber collapsed from exhaustion, the Comanche would be upon them that much faster.

"All right," Bell said. "For a bit."

With Webber's gun in his saddle bags, Bell decided to toss the bags over his own shoulder. He also took the Henry rifle out of the scabbard and toted it. Satisfied that Webber wouldn't have access to a weapon, Bell helped him step into the saddle.

Sleeping in the saddle is a skill hard to pick up for the unaccustomed. Bell had learned in the War of the Rebellion how to doze in the saddle on extended, over-night marches. He'd gotten pretty good at it. But Webber's experience in the 9th Cavalry had not taught him the art. The poor man kept nodding off, he'd start to feel like he was falling, and he start awake, only to repeat the pattern over and over.

***

The morning sun was getting hot as it rose higher in the sky. Bell found he was going to his canteen too often, which meant he'd not drank enough the day before.

The Brazos River flows north before cutting east and then dropping south, and Bell's hope was to hit it early in the afternoon just about the spot where it bends east.

But going through the night and only being able to guess how far they'd traveled, he wasn't sure where or when they would arrive at the river. If they got it at the east bend, they would still have about a hundred miles to go to get to Jacksboro and Fort Richardson. But traveling at night, Bell had lost all sense of time and direction, and he did not know how much farther they had to go to get to the Brazos River or if they would even find it where he expected to.

Webber's sleep came in such fits and starts that Bell didn't mind letting him go on like that for a while. With Comanche warriors on their backtrail, Bell wanted both of them as rested, as watered, and as fed as they could possibly be.

By noon, Webber was walking again.

"It's not exactly refreshing, sleeping on the back of a horse. But I suppose I feel some better," he said. "Where are you from, Deputy U.S. Marshal Jack Bell?"

"I've got a place up in Two Rivers Station."

"I ain't never heard of that. Whereabouts is it?"

"On the Red River. Straight north from Dallas."

"All right. We came through Dallas on the way to Fort Richardson. I know where Dallas is. So, on the Red River, you must be right up there across the river from Indian Territory."

"Yep."

"Maybe I should have run to the Territory. They say a man can get lost up there among the Injuns."

"Probably so. If you'd gotten far into the Territory, it would have been damn hard to find you."

"If my horse hadn't give out, you think you'd have caught me?"

"Private Webber, you leave a pretty big trail. Burned out campfires. Horse droppings. Prints in the sand. Broken mesquite branches. I didn't want to have to chase you up into the Staked Plain, and I can't say what might have happened if you'd gotten there. But you were easy to track."

"What if I'd gone up into Indian Territory?"

"You'd have been harder to find, I'll say that. Especially if you went into a big town for a day and didn't let nobody see you leave. Do that a couple of times, and it'd be nothing less than a miracle to track you. Men think running off into the wilds is the way to get away. Hell, I ain't no good at tracking, but I can follow a man out through the plains without much trouble. But you go into a town where they's a hundred different tracks being made every day, and slip out without anybody seeing which direction you went, and it'd be impossible to find you."

"So if you was on the dodge, that's what you'd do?"

"Sure. Ride into Indian Territory. Go through forests and streams. Take a well-traveled road full of tracks. Veer off that road into a forest. Find another road. Ride into a town. Stay overnight, and in the middle of the night slip out of town. Do that again. Maybe a third time. Different towns, different points on the compass. Always being careful that you don't give a clue to someone who might later be questioned by a lawman. Then ride off somewhere a long ways away where don't nobody know you. And you change your name, keep your nose clean, and don't give the local law reason to look twice at you. If I had to run, that's how I'd do it."

"I wish now that's how I'd done it," Webber said, chuckling to himself. "I sure do. Wouldn't be out in this heat, with my hands chained, and them Comanche trying to kill me."

"Yep," Bell said. "I wish that how you'd done it, too. I'd chase you for a couple of months, maybe, and stay in hotel rooms or camp near rivers. Would have been easier on me, too."

They walked on for a bit, but Webber went to talking again.

"Two Rivers Station, huh? You got a family there?"

"A wife, twin boys."

"Oh yeah? How old are them boys?"

"Just turned two years old a couple of months ago."

"I bet they are a mess," Webber laughed. "Your poor wife. I bet she is plumb haggard."

"She's got her mama and her grandmother nearby to help."

"You miss her, or you glad to get out of that house?"

"I miss her," Bell said. "I prefer waking up next to her over waking up next to this horse."

He reached out and gave Petey a pat on the neck, and the horse snorted back at him.

"I could use a drank o' water," Webber said.

They stopped and Bell gave some of his water to Webber. He poured some into his hat and held it for Petey. If they didn't soon come to the Brazos, Bell was going to run out of water and the Comanche would seem like a smaller problem.

There was a tall hill a couple of hundred yards to the north.

"You go on and keep walking," Bell said. "I'm going to ride up to that hill yonder and see if I can see the Brazos. I'm hoping we ain't far from it. I'll be back with you in just a minute."

Webber set out east again, and Bell stepped into the saddle. After a day of walking, Petey seemed delighted to be able to run for a minute, and they made the distance up to the top of the hill very quickly. Bell put his eyes on Webber to be sure the man wasn't trying some foolish thing, but Webber was just walking. Bell stretched as tall as he could in the saddle and looked out to the south and east. If the Brazos River was out there, Bell couldn't see it. Although he did think, maybe, there was way off in the distance a line of cottonwoods, and if that was what he saw, then it would be the Brazos. It gave him some hope.

But all that hope evaporated when Bell looked back west. A small dust cloud way off in the distance was moving at a fast pace. It had to be the Comanche, and they were coming on at such a rate that Bell understood they were not interested in playing any more games. They weren't going to shadow Bell and Webber. They weren't going to lie in wait and ambush. They weren't going to save an attack until after dark. They had discovered the tracks that would lead them to Bell and Webber, and they were coming fast to overtake their prey. The hornets intended to sting.

"Damn," Bell muttered to the horse.

Half a mile in front of Webber there was a small rise, not even as big as the hill Bell was on now. But it was a rise all the same. It was pretty well covered in low mesquite, and it presented an opportunity.

"Private Webber!" Bell yelled out. "Run for that hill!"

Webber turned and looked behind him. He was too low to see the dust cloud on the horizon, but he didn't wait to see it. He understood the meaning behind Bell's order.

Bell watched the dust cloud. Maybe they'd have half an hour before the Comanche were upon them.

Bell snapped the reins, and Petey took off at a run. They passed Webber, but Bell did not slow down. When he reached the top of the hill, he dismounted and led Petey a ways down the back side. The only advantage he could arrange was surprise, so he tied Petey to a mesquite tree where on the back side of the hill the horse would be hidden from the Comanche.

Bell took Webber's pistol out of the saddlebag and turned the cylinder to be sure it was loaded. He put caps on all but the last chamber. He also checked the caps on his own revolver and dropped it back into his holster. And then he scurried back up to the top of the hill, just in time to watch Webber get to the top.

"They coming?" Webber asked, breathing hard and near to collapsing.

"They are. Hold your wrists out."

Webber eyed his gun in Bell's hand. "You going to give me that?"

"I am."

"You ain't worried I'll shoot you and steal your horse?"

"The thought has crossed my mind," Bell said. "But I can't fight off these Indians without putting a gun in your hand, and I can't run without leaving you here. I ain't going to leave you, so I suppose I'd rather take my chances with you than with them."

Bell unlocked the chains on Webber's wrist and handed him over the Colt six-shooter.

"My hope is to take them by surprise," Bell said. "Let them ride up pretty close to us. I'll give them what I can with the rifle, but we don't go to pistols until they're in easy shooting distance. If we ain't killed all of them by the time we have to reload, we'll never get out of here. So don't pull that trigger unless you know you're going to get one."

Webber's face was tight with anxiety.

"Other than riding down on that camp of women and children, you ever get in a battle?" Bell asked.

"No, sir," Webber said.

Bell clenched his jaw. "Don't shoot until you can hit them. But don't hesitate to shoot when the time comes."

"Yes, sir," Webber said, though Bell still had his doubts.

They both knelt down behind the mesquite trees. They would not provide any kind of breastwork that would lend protection from bullets, but Bell's hope was the Comanche would not know they were riding into an ambush until the first shot was fired.

The dust cloud grew visible. And then it grew larger as the Comanche approached. They were coming at a good pace, obviously believing they were close to their prey. But before they were in sight, the cloud settled a bit.

"They've slowed down," Webber said.

"Can't run their horses but so long. They're still coming."

The half hour Bell expected turned into nearly an hour long wait. Webber drank the last of what Bell had poured into his canteen, and Bell's canteen was mighty low.

And then they saw the Comanche. It was the same band of warriors Bell had seen the previous day. Twenty-one Comanche, all mounted. Their horses were at a walk, and the Comanche were spread out. It wasn't going to be easy fighting them like that. Bunched up, a couple of shots into the body of the group were likely to hit something worthwhile. But spread out, they made for many difficult targets instead of one easy target.

Bell had hit targets at almost eight hundred yards with the Henry rifle, but those were stationary targets where he'd had plenty of time to aim. So he wanted the Indians nearer to him than that before he opened fire. He was sure that if he and Webber were coming off the plains alive, they'd have to put down this entire band of Comanche. And he wouldn't do that if they were just barely in range when he started shooting. So he steadied his breathing and waited as they approached. He kept the rifle down, too. Pretty as it was with the gleaming brass receiver, Bell knew the brass of the Henry rifle would gleam like a lighthouse as soon as he raised it up.

The Comanche were within five hundred yards when Webber whispered, "How much closer you going to let them get?"

"A bit," Bell said.

At three hundred yards, Bell started picking his first

couple of targets, but he'd not yet raised the rifle.

In the war, his men called Jack Bell "Hell's Bell" because of the ferocity with which he fought. Jack Bell took no pride in his ability to kill men. It's a thing that haunted his dreams. But with a band of Comanche warriors just two hundred yards away, he didn't mind so much that he'd built a reputation among his men as a killer. He planned to rely heavily upon the skills that built that reputation in just a few moments.

At one hundred and fifty yards, Bell swung the Henry rifle up to his shoulder, adjusted the iron ladder sight to take aim at the Comanche he'd decided would be the first man to die, and Hell's Bell pulled the trigger.

The big rifle boomed death across the plain, and Private Clifton Webber was in awe to see one of the Comanche drop from his saddle.

Bell dropped the lever, shifted the rifle and before any of the Comanche had time to process what had happened, he put his sight on the next warrior. Death boomed again.

Now they came, with a ferocious battle cry, urging their horses to close the distance.

Bell shot a third man. He was working his way among the easy targets, those nearest and presenting the biggest target. Webber was getting anxious, and he raised up the Colt.

"Not yet!" Bell shouted at him through the ringing in their ears. The Henry spit fire and hell, and a fourth Comanche dropped. The lever fell, the spent shell ejected, the trigger pulled. Hell's Bell was fast with the rifle. His next shot hit a horse but left the rider intact.

"Damnation," Bell cursed. He hated to shoot a horse.

The Comanche warriors fanned out. Hell's Bell shot another, and unhorsed another. The Comanche were riding to get at both flanks. Bell focused on those riding to his left. They were harder to hit now, and his next shot missed. He shot a third horse through the neck, and he saw the rider get trapped when the horse went down. A man trapped under a horse was just as good as a dead man. Bell aimed for the horses and found them to be easier targets.

He'd fired twelve of his sixteen and all but one hit a rider or a horse. Those Comanche who had tried to get at his left flank were wheeling and riding away, but those coming at the hill from Bell's right were damn close. Bell drew the Colt revolver from its holster.

"Now!" Bell said, startled that Webber had not yet fired a shot.

There were six or seven, maybe eight, riding up the hill on the right. The closest of the warriors leapt off his horse, a spear in hand, and charged at Bell and Webber. He was just feet away.

Webber fired and missed, but Bell had the Colt up and hit the man in the chest, knocking him off his feet. Two more were off their horses and charging. Bell thumbed back the hammer on the Colt and fired, but missed both of them. Webber fired and hit one square in the chest. Bell fired and winged the other man. The Comanche spun and started fleeing in the other direction.

Webber fired and hit a horse and the beast bucked and threw its rider and stamped several times before collapsing.

From the corner of his eye, Bell spotted a rider who'd gotten in behind them and was riding toward Petey, obviously planning to take the horse. Bell raised up the Henry and fired and the Comanche fell from the horse with a hole in his stomach.

Those warriors still mounted were reining up and wheeling their horses. Webber was trying to get a shot off, but he couldn't find the aim. Finally he did and hit a horse in the hind quarter, but the horse kept running.

Bell returned to the Henry rifle.

The Comanche who could were fleeing off to the west. Bell sighted the one who was in the lead – the one farthest away – and pulled the trigger on the Henry. The Comanche took the shot in his shoulder and fell forward, but he managed to stay on his horse.

"We did it!" Webber shouted. "We did it!"

Bell felt the elation but didn't give voice to it. He'd been fairly certain they were going to be killed.

All around them was carnage. Dead and dying horses and shot Comanche littered the ground around the hill. The mesquite trees in front of where Bell and Webber made their stand were littered with arrows, and Bell discovered the sleeve of his shirt was torn where an arrow had passed through it.

A couple of the men who'd been unhorsed but otherwise not harmed were running to the west, fleeing with the others. But one of Comanche was charging up the hill. Webber cocked back the hammer of the Colt, took a steady aim, and shot the man dead.

Two unhorsed Comanche were trying to free one of the braves who'd been trapped under his own horse. Bell raised up the Henry and shot over their heads, and they both scrambled away, leaving their comrade still trapped and struggling under the dead horse.

"Now we did it," Bell said. But when he turned, Clifton Webber had cocked back the hammer on the Colt and had it leveled at the deputy marshal.

"Put down them guns Deputy Bell," Webber said. "I don't want to shoot you. But I'll do it if I have to. I done killed a man once to get away, and I'll do it again."

Jack Bell sighed heavy. "Throw it down, Clifton," he said. "You ain't going to shoot me."

Webber bit his lip. "I don't want to. But I will."

"The gun's empty," Bell said. "You fired all six of your shots."

"I fired five," Webber said. "I counted 'em. I planned the last one for you. I ain't going to be hanged."

"Throw it down."

Webber pulled the trigger and the hammer fell, but the Colt did not fire. Webber looked down at the gun, astonished.

He never saw Hell's Bell swing the rifle, and when the butt of the Henry smashed into the side of his head, Webber blacked out before he hit the ground.

***

"You sure did hit me though," Webber chuckled, and his laugh made Bell smile. Whatever else Clifton Webber was, he was too damned congenial for Bell to stay angry at him.

"You never should have drawed down on me," Bell

said. "You're lucky all I did was hit you."

Webber was mounted on one of the Comanche horses that Bell had rounded up. His wrists were back in chains, and Bell had tied him to the horse. They were both mounted now and riding along beside the Brazos River at an easy pace. Including the horse Webber was on, they were bringing five Comanche horses back with them.

"I'm sorry about that," Webber said. "I didn't want to shoot you. But I don't want to get hanged, neither. That was smart of you to remove the cap on the last chamber, though. But what if I'd tried to fire that on the Comanche?"

"I figured if it came down to your last shot, I'd be dead already anyway. And then I wouldn't much care what happened to you."

Webber laughed. "Yes, sir, Deputy Bell, you're a smart man. A smart man who hits hard."

"When we get back to the fort, I'm going to testify for you," Bell said. "I don't know what good it'll do, but I'm going to tell them that you had the opportunity to shoot me and get away, and you didn't do it."

"But I tried," Webber said.

Bell nodded. "You could have shot me when I handed you that Colt, gotten on my horse and ran. You waited it out, fought the Comanche with me, and you didn't try to get away until it was over. Fact is, I like you well enough. I've arrested a lot of outlaws and troublemakers, and most of them are ornery and deserve what's coming to them. But I have some sympathy for you. I don't think you meant to kill that corporal, and it ain't your fault that you ain't cut out for the army."

"I hate for you to delay going home on my account,"

Webber said. "But if you can keep the army from hanging me, I'd be much obliged."

***

The three officers who sat the court martial at Fort Richardson were all Yankee veterans, and while they were interested in hearing about the fight with the Comanche, they didn't much care that a Confederate cavalryman thought they should spare the life of a private who deserted his post and killed a corporal.

They quickly came to the judgement that Private Clifton Webber should hang for his crimes.

Jack Bell was disappointed but not surprised when the court martial was finished by late morning and its verdict declared. Webber was removed to the four-foot by eight-foot cell in the guardhouse to wait out the numbered days of his life.

Major Bacon, one of the officers who sat on the court, invited Bell to stay on another night at the fort, but Bell declined.

"Sooner I leave, the sooner I can get home to my wife," Bell explained. "But I would like to say a farewell to the prisoner, if you don't mind."

Major Bacon, who was probably a Union man anyway, pointed Bell in the direction of the guardhouse.

There were four cells in the stone guardhouse, and all four were occupied. Webber, the only man confined under a sentence of death, was in a cell by himself, though the other three cells all held two men each.

When Bell walked into the guardhouse he arrived just in time to see the two guards, both armed with carbines, lock Webber into his cell. Bell waited for the guards in the office. He recognized both guards as having been in the court martial. They were both young, white boys. Neither of them were old enough to have been in the war. New recruits put on guard duty.

They came into the office and stored the rifles. One of the guards stepped into the guard quarters and lounged on a bed where he picked up a book. The other guard sat down at the desk and set the key to the cell on top of the desk. The desk was crowded with papers where the guard was writing what appeared to be a letter home. Bell assumed the boy had started the letter in the morning, before the court martial, and was planning to get back to it now. In addition to the papers, there was also a box of pencils and a knife on the desk. There was also a copy of Harper's on the desk.

Bell sat down on the edge of the desk and picked up the copy of Harper's. He thumbed through it for a couple of seconds. The boy sitting behind the desk just watched him.

"You in the war, son?" Bell asked.

"No, sir," the boy said, wondering what was happening.

"I rode with Stuart," Bell said.

"In the Confederacy?" the boy asked, and his voice rose.

"Yep. And now I'm a United States Deputy Marshal. It's a strange world, but it's the one we've got."

"Stuart was a good cavalryman," the boy conceded.

"Yes he was," Bell said.

Bell carelessly tossed the Harper's magazine back

onto the desk. Then he stood up and leaned forward, placing both palms flat on the desk and leaned forward.

"Your prisoner in there, he's condemned to die. But I took a liking to him, even though I had to bring him in. I hope, with him being colored and in a cell, that you'll still treat him decent."

"I'll treat him like any other prisoner," the guard said, and the confused look on his face wasn't changed none.

"That's all I can ask," Bell said. "That, and maybe sneak him an extra piece of bacon or two at suppertime. Man's final days ought to be as comfortable as possible."

The guard's face reddened. "I ain't sneaking nobody no bacon."

Bell smiled. He closed his palms on the desk so that he was now leaning on his knuckles.

"Well, if you change your mind, I'd appreciate him getting an extra piece of bacon. Cornbread? Do y'all have good cornbread here?"

"We get biscuits that are tolerable," the guard said.

"Maybe an extra piece of bacon or two and an extra one of them good biscuits. It'd be a kindness."

Bell stood up straight.

"Major Bacon said it'd be all right for me to say farewell to the private."

"Sure," the guard said. "I don't care none."

Bell walked back to the cells. They were a typical sort of holding cell with several round, iron bars running vertical and a couple of flat, horizontal bars. Bell put his palms flat on the flat, horizontal bar that ran even with his chest.

"Just wanted to say farewell to you, Clifton," Bell said.

Webber, who'd been sitting on his bunk, stood up and walked toward the bars.

"I wish I could say it was a pleasure to know you," Webber said. "Maybe you'd be all right under different circumstances."

Bell laughed. "Well, it was a pleasure to know you. I wish the court martial had turned out different."

"We both knowed how it would turn out," Webber said. "You riding on?"

"I am," Bell said. "I'm tired of waking up next to my horse when I know my wife is at home."

Webber studied Bell in silence for several moments.

"It must be a hard thing," Webber said.

"What's that?"

"Putting on a badge for a government you hate." Webber put no malice in the accusation. More than anything, it just sounded like curiosity.

Bell shrugged but did not answer.

"Why you do it?" Webber persisted.

Bell knew the answer. His indecision was in whether or not he was going to give it. But after a moment, he said, "Life out here gets pretty rough. All a man's really got is his friends and his family. I suppose when I put on this badge, I don't think much on the government it represents. I just think about those friends and my family, and I wear it for them."

Bell lifted his hand from the crossbar of the jail cell. Where his hand had been, there was now a key, lifted from the guard's desk. Webber saw it but said nothing he just smiled that big toothy grin of his and started chuckling at Bell, that same infectious laugh Bell had heard so many times over the last couple of days. Webber dropped his hand over the crossbar, hiding the key in his palm.

"You are a strange man, Deputy United States Marshal Jack Bell," Clifton Webber said, shaking his head and grinning.

***

Jack Bell was sitting on the floor of his home. His sons Samuel and Richard were wrestling with him in the way that little boys wrestle with their daddies. Honor was fixing supper, and ignoring her boys. Jack had Samuel lifted into the air above his head, and Richard was trapped under his legs. And Willow, the black Labrador, was playfully pawing at Richard's head so that Richard was squealing with laughter.

Despite the noises from the boys, Bell heard the sound of a rider through the open windows. It was still daylight, but from the floor, Bell could not see out the window to know who was there.

"Jack Bell!" he heard someone call. "It's Tubby! Need a word with you!"

Jack set Samuel down on the sofa and let Richard up, and then Bell stood up and walked outside.

Bell was one of two deputy U.S. Marshals serving under Zeke Thornton up at Two Rivers Station. The other was Minko, a full-blooded Chickasaw from up in the territory. Bell, who owned the ferry at Two Rivers, employed some of Minko's relatives to run the ferry and look after his herd of cattle. Tubby was one of Minko's cousins who usually worked as a cowpuncher.

Bell opened the front door. Tubby was still mounted but had ridden up to the front of the house.

"Howdy Jack," Tubby said. "I wasn't sure you was back yet. They said you'd gone chasing a fugitive out west."

"Just got back yesterday," Bell said. "Everything all right?"

"I was working the ferry today," Tubby said. "My cousin Tom was feeling poorly, so I said I'd work the ferry for a couple of days."

Bell shrugged. So long as the cattle didn't wander off and the ferry transported paying customers to and fro over the river, Bell didn't much care who worked where.

"Anyway, so I was down at the ferry, and I just took a fellow across. He didn't have no money, but he said he was a friend of yours."

"Is that right?" Jack asked suspiciously.

"Colored fellow. Said for me to give you this."

Tubby tossed something, and Bell grabbed it out of the air. Bell immediately recognized the key to the cell at Fort Richardson's guardhouse.

"He said for me to tell you that he was heading up into the Territory. Plans to go to a town or two and hopes to get lost."

Bell looked at the key in his hand and chuckled to

himself.

When Bell's parents first came to Texas when he was just a boy, the place was already hard. Weather beaten, teeming with dangers, and big as the outdoors, the West had a way of attracting folks who set the rules they lived by, and those rules didn't always match up well with the rules of the next man. But since the war, life itself was sold cheap by those men who made their own rules.

Private Clifton Webber had sold another man's life cheap because Webber couldn't live under other men's rules.

Bell felt pretty certain that Webber should pay for his crimes and, because of Bell, had escaped making that payment. But at the same time, Jack Bell had his own rules, too. And one of those rules stated pretty clear that if a man stands beside you in a battle, that man is your friend. And friends, as hard as they may be to have, do for one another.

Honor walked out onto the front porch and looked at the key in Jack's hand.

"What is that?" she asked.

"I ain't sure," Bell said. "Maybe it's justice. Or maybe it's a criminal who's waiting for justice to catch up to him. But it means that fellow I chased out across the plains is on the dodge again."

"Oh, Jack, please tell me you ain't going after him again. You just got home."

"Naw," Bell said. "If a U.S. Marshal needs to chase after that boy, it'll have to be someone other than me. He's going to be a damn sight tougher to find this time around."

THE TOWN MARSHAL

Zeke Thornton rode into the little Texas town expecting trouble.

The federal judge in Sherman, Daniel Fitzsimmons, called the place Sorrel Creek when he handed Zeke the warrant with the name Billy Chandler on it. Fitzsimmons told Zeke to bring Chandler back to Sherman to face trial.

"He shot and killed two deputy marshals who were transporting his cousin to a federal penitentiary," Fitzsimmons explained. "One of the deputy marshals, mortally wounded but not dead, shot the cousin. The cousin is dead. But this Billy Chandler, he rode off and got away. Don't kill him, Zeke. Bring him back here to me so I can hang him. I knew both them deputy marshals."

Zeke had spent the last couple of weeks sitting behind a desk in Sherman doing paperwork for the Marshal Service. It always happened around court week that Zeke had to ride down out of Two Rivers Station and do the tiresome duties associated with his badge – seeing to the jurors, transporting prisoners, protecting the court proceedings, and bringing in reluctant witnesses. He had a couple of part time deputies in Sherman who helped him with such matters, but as the U.S. Marshal for the northern district of Texas, it was Zeke's responsibility to be present for court week.

But on the fourth day of a session that looked to be going into two weeks, Fitzsimmons handed Zeke the warrant. "Your deputies can transport prisoners. You go and get this fugitive."

Zeke set out for Sorrel Creek right away, but he sent word up to Two Rivers Station, to his full time deputies, Jack Bell and Minko, and asked that they ride to Sorrel Creek to help him.

An outlaw brave enough to gun down two deputy U.S. Marshals might be more than Zeke cared to deal with on his own, especially if the judge wanted him brought in alive.

Sorrel Creek was far enough out on the frontier that Zeke kept alert for Indian attack on the ride west. Comanche raiding parties were occasionally active on the plains, but Zeke had not heard of any recent Indian troubles.

"Of course, when you don't hear of them for a while, that's when you need to start worrying," he confided to his horse.

Like most men who rode the lonely plains, Zeke had a habit of talking to his horse, a pretty chestnut with a lighter mane and tail that almost looked like blonde hair. She was a lovely Morgan horse, and Jack Bell and Minko often teased Zeke Thornton, a bachelor, that the horse Sandy was his "blonde-headed wife."

Sorrel Creek was far enough north that it was hilly country dotted with clusters of cottonwoods along the creeks and bottoms, and it was a pleasant ride out to Sorrel Creek. He crossed over a well-worn cattle trail and camped beside a pleasant little stream. It was springtime, so the night was not too cold and the day was not too hot, and Zeke Thornton thought this was not a bad way to live a life.

But when he topped the hill overlooking the town, Zeke had a pit in his stomach. From his vantage point on the hill overlooking the town, Zeke counted two hotels, three saloons, a couple of supply stores, a smithy and two liveries. There were a dozen houses, a bakery, and not far out of town along the banks of a little river there was a gristmill. What he did not see was a steeple of any kind, and a town that lacked a church was bound to be a rough place.

All the same, it was a pretty spot. The town was quaint, and the river that ran west of the town supplied the precious water necessary for a large stand of big hardwoods to be growing all down along the river near the gristmill. It made for a very pastoral picture looking down on it from the nearby hill.

Zeke slid his Colt revolver from its holster and checked the cylinder to be sure all six chambers were loaded, and a turned the cylinder to make sure he had caps on each chamber.

"All right, Sandy girl, let's go see what we can get into," Zeke said, and he squeezed his leg's on the Morgan's ribs and she galloped down the path into town.

Zeke's first stop was to the small office in town with the "Constable" sign hanging above it. He figured if Billy Chandler was a local bad man, the constable would know where to find him.

The constable's office was a decent sized structure, but when Zeke went inside he could see that it not only housed an office and two jail cells, but there was also a room attached that served as living quarters for the town marshal.

The man seated at the desk had a glass of whiskey in his hand and had the glass halfway to his mouth when Zeke opened up the door. Zeke couldn't suppress a frown when he saw the man – a huge potbelly prevented the town marshal from getting too close to his paperwork, his clothes were shabby and dirty, his hair was fleeing the top of his head, and he had a salt-and-pepper beard with wire hairs going off in every direction.

Worse, though, than his general appearance was the bleary look in his eye.

"You the town marshal?" Zeke asked, shutting the door behind him.

"I ain't," the man said, and brought his glass the rest of the way to his lips and took a big drink.

"Well, who are you?" Zeke asked.

"Who's asking?" the man retorted.

"My name's Zeke Thornton. I'm a United States Marshal. I'm looking for town constable. Sign out front seemed to indicate this might be where I'd find him."

"You'll find him in the cemetery," the bleary-eyed man said. "Shot dead last week in a gunfight out front of the Globe."

"Who are you?"

"I'm the town's deputy marshal," the man said, taking another drink from his glass.

"You're the deputy marshal?" Zeke asked doubtfully.

"I am."

"What did you do about the man that shot the town marshal?" Zeke asked.

"What do you mean?"

"Is he in your jail?"

The man took another drink from the glass and leaned back in his chair. "Who are you?"

Zeke sighed and shook his head. "I just answered you that. I'm a U.S. Marshal. Name is Zeke Thornton."

"Oh, yeah."

A man in Texas in the 1860s became adept at talking to men who'd had too much whiskey, and this wasn't the first time Zeke Thornton had attempted to get information from a drunken man.

"I'm looking for Billy Chandler," Zeke said. "You know him?"

"Youngest of the Chandler boys," the deputy marshal answered. "Sure I know him. If you're looking for him, you better hope you don't find him."

"Why is that?" Zeke asked.

"Chandler boys are who shot the Marshal Roberts."

"That the town marshal you said was killed last week?"

"That's right."

"So you know who shot Marshal Roberts, and you're the deputy marshal for this town, and you haven't don't anything about it?"

"I ain't going after the Chandler boys. I like livin' too much. Who did you say you are?"

Zeke rubbed his chin and looked at the ceiling. He was pretty convinced this conversation wasn't going to help him any. "How much of that bottle have you had to drink today?"

The deputy marshal looked at the bottle for a moment. "When I started drinking, it was up to here," he said, pointing to the top of the bottle. Then he slid his finger down the length of the bottle to the top of the whiskey, which was nearly to the bottom. "And now it's here. So I guess I drank that much of it."

"Is there someone in this town who might have some answers but has not had that much whiskey?" Zeke asked. "A mayor, or an alderman?"

The deputy marshal turned the bottle upside down and poured the last of the whiskey into his glass.

"Down at the Globe," he said. "Carson. He owns the place. He's on the town council."

"Obliged," Zeke said.

He shook his head in wonder at a deputy marshal sitting drunk in the office with the town marshal still fresh six feet underground.

Zeke stepped back into the saddle and walked Sandy through the one road in town until he came to an eatery and saloon with the name "Globe" carved into a wooden sign hanging out front. The hitch post was crowded with horses, and Zeke figured the eating must be good.

Inside nearly all the tables were full. All the patrons

were dusty men, cowpunchers and hardworking men from the mill or the stores. But at one table, beside the front window, sat a well-dressed man, clean and fresh shaved.

Zeke walked over to him. "You Carson?" Zeke asked.

The man took a hard look at Zeke, from boots to hat he looked him over. "Don't think we've met before," he said. "My name's Tim Carson."

"Name is Zeke Thornton. I'm a United States Marshal. Mind if I have a seat?"

Carson held out an open hand toward the chair across the table. "Please."

Zeke pulled out the chair and sat. Carson had the appearance of a man who was living well. Older, with gray hair and a gray trimmed beard, he wasn't overweight but obviously wasn't missing meals, neither. His face was tan, but not leathery like so many of the cowpunchers eating at his tables.

"Marshal Thornton, if I was you, I don't believe I'd wear that badge where it's quite so obvious. Unfortunately, here in Sorrel Creek, lawmen don't last very long."

Zeke nodded his head. "So I've heard. Town marshal was shot last week?"

"That's right," Carson said. "They shot Marshal Roberts in the street right out front of the Globe, here. That what you're here about?"

"I'm in town looking for Billy Chandler."

Tim Carson started and looked around the room. He leaned forward across the table. "Listen here, Marshal Thornton, I'm going to have to ask you to either take off that badge and put it in your pocket or find someplace else to sit. You come in here asking questions about one of the Chandlers, and you're wearing that badge, and it makes me nervous I'll get shot in the crossfire."

Zeke smiled, but he realized Tim Carson was serious. "You ain't joking," Zeke said.

"Not at all."

Zeke covered his badge with his duster, then slipped it off his vest and dropped it in the watch pocket. "Better?" he asked.

"I appreciate that," Carson said. "Now maybe we can talk in peace."

"Are some of the Chandlers in here?" Zeke asked.

"Oh, no," Carson said. "But a fair number of these boys have rode with them, and anyone in here would be glad to let them know I was talking about them with a lawman."

"Well, I'm looking for Billy."

"You find him, and you'll find the rest of them. There's eight of them. Some of them are brothers, some are cousins. I couldn't tell you which is a brother and which is a cousin. They showed up here two years ago, all come out of the war. They built a little shack up in the hills. Took to rustling cattle, robbing stages. They come to town once in a while, get drunk, get in a fight, and most times end up shooting some damn fool who doesn't have sense enough to stay wide of 'em. Most everybody in Sorrel Creek is scared of them. The ones who ain't scared of them end up contributing to the census of the graveyard north of town."

"Sounds like a wonderful situation for building a prosperous town," Zeke said.

"Most everybody here can claim to have shot a man while drunk. Sorrel Creek is a rough place, Marshal. We need law, but we've had three town marshals in the last two years, and all three of them are currently resting peacefully under a headstone. Our deputy marshal is only part time, because the rest of the time he's working as the town drunk. I built this place back in '58, and I did well for three years. During the war, the town just sort of held on and waited. A lot of folks left to go with Hood. Then after the war, Sorrel Creek had a knack for attracting rough men. Veterans, mostly, who couldn't go back to living among decent folks, so they came out here to live with the cows out on the range. I should have sold out and moved when our original town marshal quit the job, but I wasn't as quick to see what was happening as he was."

"Where's he now?" Zeke asked.

"That's him sitting at the back table over there," Carson said, nodding toward a man seated alone.

The man looked to be just shy of fifty years old. He was obviously a strong man, well-built with a hard jawline. The word "grizzled" came to Zeke's mind. The man sat quietly, alone at his table and intent on his food.

"Josh Becker. Came here in '56 to build the grist mill. He was the town marshal when I got here, and back then the town was pretty quiet, like I said. Mostly, he just took the drunks down to the jail to let them sleep it off. But nobody did much of anything because they knew Marshal Becker was strong as an ox and fast as a rattler."

Zeke couldn't understand how a lawman could live in a lawless town. "It don't bother him how things are?"

"It bothers him. It bothers me, as an alderman. But what's he going to do? Pick a fight with the Chandler in front of him and get hisself shot in the back by the three or four standing behind him?"

"What about the sheriff?" Zeke asked.

"The sheriff is sixty miles east of here. He ain't ever even been to Sorrel Creek. Hell, there's not three men out of ten in this town could even tell you what county we live in. What we need is the damned Reconstruction Government to send the army here, but they won't do nothing for us. Only thing gets them to lift of a finger is if we got Indian raids or coloreds that can't vote. And we haven't had an Indian raid since before the war, and there ain't but two families of coloreds here, and after the army come through and threatened us, we let them vote now."

Zeke looked across the restaurant. Every man he could see was wearing a six-shooter, and some of them were wearing two.

"So what do you want with Billy Chandler?" Carson asked.

"I've got a warrant for him," Zeke said. "He shot and killed a couple of federal marshals."

Carson blew out his breath and frowned. "Well, I can't say I envy you none. I sure hope I ain't around when you go to serve that warrant."

Just then a big, grimy looking man who'd been beaten by weather stood up from a table across the dining room. He made a commotion when he did it, and Zeke turned in his seat to see what the noise was about.

"Larry Murray!" the big man shouted. He was looking at the door where a tall, thin man had just walked in. "I told you not to let me see you again!"

The big man started pushing his way past the other tables. The man he was talking to – Larry Murray – stood his ground and reached for his six shooter.

"Not in here!" Carson shouted, and he leapt up from the table with a pepperbox pistol in his hand. "Y'all take your business outside."

Larry Murray, without turning his back on the big man, stepped backwards outside the door he'd just come through.

"Here you go, Marshal," Carson said. "You want to see what kind of town we've got, you're about to have a view of it. The big fellow there is Carlos Santos. He's meaner than a bag of rattlesnakes."

The big man never broke stride. He walked outside, and several of the diners, including Zeke and Carson, followed him.

Murray had backed up into the road, and the big man, Carlos Santos, followed him into the street.

"You got your hand on your gun, Larry," Santos said. "Why don't you draw it?"

Murray's voice quavered, and Zeke knew right away which man of the two would win the gun fight.

"I ain't got no quarrel with you," Murray said.

"You said I was rustling your herd," Santos said. "So why don't you do something about it?"

Murray's hand moved from his gun to his belt buckle. He pulled it loose so that the gun and holster fell into the dirt. "I'm unarmed," Murray said. "I ain't going to fight you, Santos."

"Well that's just going to make it easy," Santos said.

His right hand dropped to the grip of his six-shooter.

Zeke was standing on the plank sidewalk in front of the restaurant. He glanced left and right at the other spectators and could not believe no man among them was going to intervene.

Zeke's Colt was out of its holster and he took three big steps off the sidewalk and out into the street. Santos, watching Murray, didn't see Zeke coming. Zeke swung the heavy barrel of the Colt and caught Santos in the side of the head. He expected the big man would be staggered, but Santos merely shook his head and spun on his heel to face Zeke.

"Who the hell are you?" Santos asked, and seeing the Colt in Zeke's hand, he started to draw his own revolver.

Zeke punched Santos as hard as he could in the nose with the butt of the revolver, and now the big man stumbled backwards. A cheer went up from the men on the sidewalk.

"Draw that gun and I'll shoot you dead," Zeke said. "I'm a United States Marshal, and I'm arresting you."

Santos had both hands up to his nose, blood flowing like a waterfall.

"Arresting me for what?" The question came muffled from behind his hands.

"Disturbing the peace," Zeke said. "Now unlatch that belt and let that gun drop. You can sober up in the town jail."

"Like hell!" Santos said, and he dropped his right hand to the grip of his revolver.

Zeke was not more than four feet away, his revolver was already in his hand, and he was already aiming it at Santos. Without really thinking it through, Zeke felt shooting the man would be murder. So he pulled the trigger with the barrel pointing at Santos's revolver. The butt of the gun splintered, and Santos jerked his hand away like he'd been stung.

Zeke took a quick step closer to Santos and swung the revolver again, this time catching Santos with the barrel in the side of the head. A glassy stare came across Santos's face. Zeke knew he'd rung the big man's bell with that blow to the head, so he followed it up by smashing the butt of the gun into Santos's face a second time. The big man's knees wobbled, and he dropped into the street.

Zeke bent over and unloosed the man's belt, untied the holster from his thigh and slid the belt out from under him. Santos moaned but did not move. Now Zeke looked at the spectators on the sidewalk. He pointed to three of the biggest men who were looking on.

"You boys pick him up and tote him down to the city jail. Tell that worthless deputy marshal to lock him up."

Without argument, the men did what Zeke told them to do. Zeke handed the gun belt to Carson. "I suppose you can return this when he's sober."

Carson, like the other spectators, was slack jawed.

"I don't know if that was brave or stupid," Carson said. "You handle yourself well. How would you like a job?"

"I have a job," Zeke said.

"You take the town marshal badge, and I'll pay you a hundred dollars a month to clean up this town. You get a room at the marshal's office, and every meal you eat at the

Globe is free. I don't expect President Grant pays you that well."

The job offer was made with most of the spectators still looking on.

"Don't do it," one of them called out. "Town marshals don't last long around here." That set most of the men on the sidewalk to laughing and slapping each other on the back, and there were catcalls of agreement.

But a voice in the back of the crowd sounded loud over the rest of them. "You take the job, and I'll be your deputy."

The men standing in front of the voice stepped off to the side to see who'd spoke up, and when they did, Zeke saw that it was Josh Becker offering his services.

Carson's eyes were almost pleading as he nodded his head at Zeke.

"I will not keep on that worthless drunk currently identifying himself as a deputy town marshal," Zeke said.

"That's okay by me," Carson said.

"And I'll only stay so long as I have business here," Zeke said. "I'll clean up your town the best I can, but when I've got what I come for, I intend to take it and go on back to my home."

"Whatever you can do will be an improvement over our current situation," Carson said.

"All right, then," Zeke said. "I'll be your town marshal for a bit."

"I'll get the other two alderman. We'll hold an emergency meeting of the town council and make it official."

***

Zeke unsaddled Sandy and left her in the small stable out behind the town marshal's office.

Josh Becker was sitting behind the desk in the office. Carlos Santos was snoring loudly in one of the cells, and the former deputy town marshal was asleep in a separate cell, also snoring loudly.

"The town council passed an ordinance last year that requires all men in the limits of the town to be unarmed," Becker said. "That will be your most successful tool. It gives you the ability to disarm every man in whatever way necessary."

"My name's Zeke Thornton," Zeke said. "I understand you're the former town marshal."

"Josh Becker." Becker extended a hand and Zeke shook it.

"Pleasure to meet you," Zeke said.

"As I said. Your best tool is the ability to disarm men. When the town started to go to hell, I asked the alderman to pass the ordinance. They refused at the time, and so I resigned my position. They passed it last year, and asked me to come back and be marshal, but I declined."

"Why?" Zeke asked.

"Because it was too out of hand. Every damned cowpuncher, every drunk, every veteran, every passer through, every outlaw within a hundred miles of here was coming to Sorrel Creek to eat, to fornicate, and to shoot somebody. And I did not believe that a town marshal would survive the appointment."

"So what makes you think the town marshal will survive now?" Zeke asked.

"I still do not think the town marshal will survive," Becker said.

"So then why did you volunteer?"

Becker gave Zeke a hard stare. "I did not volunteer to be the town marshal," Becker said. "I volunteered to be the deputy marshal."

Zeke laughed. He put his Henry rifle up in the gun cabinet hanging on the wall beside the desk. "So you think I'll get killed, but you'll survive?"

"Yep. I figure we'll clean up the town a bit. You'll make the wrong man mad. Maybe Carlos in there, maybe the Chandler boys, maybe somebody else, and they'll come gunning for you on account of you being the marshal. And when they've killed you, I'll resign again."

Zeke grinned at the man, uncertain if he was making a poor joke or if he believed his prediction.

"Well, that's a mighty optimistic way of seeing things," Zeke said.

"I just call it like I see it," Becker said. "In the meantime, we might be able to get some of the worst of them."

"So why didn't you volunteer as deputy marshal for some of the other marshals? Way I hear it, they could have used you."

"You stepped right in and knocked down one of the

meanest sons of bitches in this town. You didn't hesitate. Those other fools they hired as marshals didn't know what they was doing. But you know how to handle yourself. If I'm going to serve as someone's deputy, it has to be someone I can trust to make it worth my while."

"And you think I can make it worth your while?"

"I do. I figure between the two of us, we can probably take down some of the roughest men, maybe enough that the others will calm down a bit."

Zeke figured Josh Becker had given thought to cleaning up the town already.

"How do you propose we do this?"

"I suppose the best way to do it is to walk into the Globe or one of the other saloons, announce yourself, and tell every man to check his weapon here at the marshal's office. Tell 'em it's the law, and you intend to enforce the law where others have failed to do."

"And you think they'll all just comply?"

"Nope. Don't think any of them will. So that's when you pick out the roughest man in the room, and either you pistol whip him like you did Carlos in there, or you shoot him out of his seat. Then they'll start to comply. Some of 'em, at least."

"Then I suppose we should get to it," Zeke said.

Becker looked past Zeke out the window. "Give it another hour. Once the sun is down they'll be more drunk. Drunker they are, the better the chance someone will pick a fight with you. That's the way we want it. Let the roughest ones come to us."

"And you're going to back me up?" Zeke asked.

"I'm backing you."

"Well, let's walk back down to the Globe. I need to get some grub before we go to disarming the town."

Josh Becker slid open the lap drawer on the wooden desk. In the top were several badges.

"I think the actual marshal badge was buried in the cemetery last week, still pinned to its previous owner," Becker said. "But these are the posse badges I used to hand out. They'll serve. I reckon it won't be long before everybody in towns knows you're the law anyway."

"I suppose you should know, I'm in town for Billy Chandler," Zeke said. "He killed two deputy U.S. Marshals. When I find him, I'll be moving on."

Becker frowned and shook his head. "That'll be a tough warrant to serve."

***

As they walked the plank sidewalk back down to the Globe, men stepped back and gave them room. Word of Zeke's showdown with Santos spread quickly in the small town, and everyone was equally interested to know that Josh Becker was again wearing a badge.

At the town marshal's office, Becker had armed up. He'd already been wearing a six shooter, but he now had two strapped to his belt in the cross-draw style. He was also toting a short, double-barrel shotgun.

Neither man spoke most of the way, but as they approached the Globe, there was a small crowd of men standing along the plank sidewalk and into the street. Unlike everyone else they'd encountered along the walk, these men did not move. The men were not speaking, and though they faced each other, all heads were turned watching the approach of the new town marshal and his deputy. Their stares were aggressive, and Zeke's eyes were scanning the men for any of them to go for a gun. He felt like he was walking into an ambush as he approached the crowd.

"Just so you boys know, the new marshal says he's going to enforce the no gun ordinance," Becker called to them. "If you're toting arms, you'd better dispossess yourself afore the marshal finishes his supper."

One of the men stepped out of the crowd and toward Zeke and Becker. Like most all the other men in town, he carried about a thick layer of dust from head to foot. He wore a bright red shirt with a light duster over it, and he had six shooters on each hip. He had a thick, bushy mustache that bounced when he spoke.

Zeke and Josh Becker both came to a stop a few feet away from the crowd of men.

"Look here, Josh," the man said. "It would be foolish for a man to go about unarmed and unable to defend hisself in this town. That's asking to get shot dead."

"Ain't nobody going to get shot if everybody's unarmed, Chuck," Becker said.

"You know as well as I do that they's folks in this town ain't going to disarm," the man said.

"Then we'll disarm them," Becker replied. Becker was like ice. His tone didn't change. He didn't get hurried or excited. Zeke liked a steady lawman, though Zeke figured it was easier for Becker to stay steady seeing as how he was standing behind Zeke. If anybody in this crowd went to shooting, Zeke would be hit first.

"Well, I ain't going to disarm," Chuck said.

Zeke decided this was as good an opportunity as any to start making a point. He dropped his hand to the grip of the revolver, and as he drew it from the holster he cocked back the hammer with his thumb. Zeke was quick with his gun, faster than most men he knew. The man Chuck was looking down the barrel of Zeke's Colt before he'd even realized that Zeke was going for the revolver.

"I'm the town marshal now, and if the law says you disarm, then by God you'll disarm. Unstrap those holsters, unloose that belt, and hand over them six shooters, or I'll see you buried with them."

The parley on the sidewalk had turned so quickly to a tense standoff that the other men in the crowd all stepped back. Becker had the shotgun up to his shoulder and both barrels looking menacing at the other men.

"Best do it, Chuck," Becker said. "Marshal's serious about his appointment. We're cleaning up this town and we're starting tonight."

Chuck's eyes shifted back and forth from Becker to the Colt.

"It ain't that I mind disarming," Chuck said. "But if you start with me, I'll be the only man in town that ain't toting protection."

"You got enemies Chuck?" Becker asked. "I've always known you to be a well-liked man. Ain't nobody going to shoot you without cause."

Chuck sniffed and bit his lip.

"All right. But you better see to your duty and

disarm everyone."

Without making any suspect movements, Chuck untied the holsters from his thighs and opened up the belt buckle. Once the guns were in Zeke's hand, Chuck stepped back into the crowd he'd been standing with. He handed the belt with the guns over to Zeke, who lowered – but did not holster – his own revolver.

Zeke was thinking about a big move. In the crowd of men who'd been standing with Chuck Zeke had counted fourteen other men.

"Now the rest of you," Zeke said, eyeing them one-by-one. "You either walk down to the marshal's office and deposit your weapons there, or you go on home and leave them. I'm going to eat my supper tonight. If I see any one of you men, after I finish eating, walking around with a gun on your hip, I'm going to suspect you of mischief. You'll be openly flaunting the law. And I ain't going to have it. This is your warning. If you're up to mischief, I'll shoot you without asking."

Zeke ran his eyes over the men, slow and steady so that they knew he was taking a mental account of their appearance.

One of the men standing safely in the back said, "I don't think the new town marshal is going to last as long as the last one."

Zeke and Josh Becker took a table at the back of the Globe, and there they both sat with their backs against the wall. Becker had eaten, so he talked while Zeke ate.

Becker recommended a bold and speedy course of action.

"If we lock up half a dozen men tonight, it'll send

the right kind of message. If we break a couple of jaws, it'll send a better message. Might even be a good idea to shoot a man or two."

"I ain't shooting a man over a no-gun ordinance," Zeke said.

"If you plan to disarm this town, you will. Some of these boys are going to be good and drunk soon. You go to disarm a drunk man, there's a good chance he'll draw on you."

"Tell me about the Chandlers. You know where their place is?"

"About twenty miles west of town, down in a holler, they've built up three little cabins. There's three brothers, Billy is the youngest. Clive and Went are his two older brothers. All three were in the war. I understand there was a fourth brother, and their pa, were both killed in the war. Besides the three brothers, there's five cousins. I couldn't tell you their names. They've all come in the last year or two."

"There may only be four cousins now," Zeke said. "When Billy Chandler killed the deputy marshals, the man he was trying to free was shot and killed."

"That may be," Josh Becker said. "They also have some women out yonder, but I don't know about them. Mostly they rustle cows. Been known to hold up a stagecoach or two. This here place is their hideout, so to speak, so they don't stir up much trouble around Sorrel Creek. They ride east to get into their real criminal activities."

"The way I hear it, they're the scourge of the town. That's the way Alderman Carson described them."

Josh Becker nodded thoughtfully. "I suppose they are. But in a town where somebody gets shot every other week, anything they do around here just ain't considered too bad a crime. If they come into town and get drunk and beat a man or shoot somebody down, nobody thinks twice about it."

Zeke watched a couple of men walk into the Globe. They both wore tall hats and menacing expressions.

"Here's trouble," Becker said. "The one on the left is Shane Duvose and the other one is a fellow named Shorty MacIntosh. They'll be looking for Paddy O'Malley over there in the corner. Paddy's married to Shane's sister, and the rumor around town yesterday was that Paddy beat her pretty good and she's laid up at Shane's house now."

As he spoke, the two men were looking around the restaurant. MacIntosh spotted O'Malley first, and he nudged Duvose and pointed to the corner where Paddy was playing cards and drinking whiskey. Paddy's back was to the door and he'd not seen the men come in.

As MacIntosh and Duvose walked toward the corner of the restaurant, the low rumble of people talking died away. The other men at the table with O'Malley looked up in the silence and saw MacIntosh and Duvose, and they slid away. O'Malley did not turn around.

From the far side of the restaurant, Tim Carson, the alderman and restaurant owner, stood up and called across the room, "Take your quarrel outside, boys! You know I don't tolerate no gun play in here."

MacIntosh turned around and looked at Carson, but Duvose kept his eyes on O'Malley's back. When MacIntosh turned, Zeke saw for the first time that both men were holding their revolvers by their sides.

"This don't concern you alderman!" MacIntosh called back at Carson.

"Outside!" Carson repeated.

Now Duvose spoke to the back of Paddy O'Malley's head. "Get up Patrick. We're going outside. No man hits my sister and gets away with it."

O'Malley sat like a statue.

"What do we do, marshal?" Becker muttered.

Zeke took one more bite of cornbread and unholstered his Colt. "I suppose you just back me up if that's what you're aiming to do."

Zeke stood up and walked between the tables toward the corner.

"MacIntosh and Duvose," he said. "I'm the new town marshal, and the law says you ain't to go around town armed. Y'all set down them guns."

Duvose, who'd not yet taken his eyes off the back of O'Malley's head, now turned and looked fire at Zeke Thornton.

"Ain't your business, marshal," Duvose said.

"Put down them guns, or it is my business."

Zeke was keeping his eyes on Duvose and MacIntosh, but he saw O'Malley turn his head slightly and look in the front window. With it growing dark outside, the window was like a mirror, and O'Malley was using it to see the men behind him.

As Zeke watched him, O'Malley drew a gun from its holster on his hip.

Now everything happened fast. O'Malley slid his chair back hard so that it toppled over onto Duvose's feet. On instinct, Duvose bent over to catch the chair. O'Malley rolled to his side, spinning and bringing up the revolver he'd slid into his hand. MacIntosh was still turned toward Carson.

The explosion of the Colt was deafening inside the restaurant. But in the close quarters, Zeke only had to fire the one shot. O'Malley howled in pain as Zeke's bullet tore into the flesh in his side. Duvose, caught off guard by the falling chair and the sudden movement from O'Malley and the boom of the Colt, tripped and fell over. MacIntosh started to raise his gun and spin back toward the fight, but Becker moved quick, stepping past a table and driving the butt of his shotgun into the side of MacIntosh's head.

Zeke took a step and planted his foot on Duvose's gun hand.

"You'll spend the night in my jail if you don't turn loose of that gun," Zeke said.

O'Malley, whose gun was on the floor, was screaming from the floor. "I'm shot! I'm dying! Somebody help me!"

"You shouldn't have hit my sister!" Duvose yelled at him. "Step off of my hand."

"Turn loose of the gun," Zeke said.

Duvose dropped the gun. Zeke kicked it to the side and then helped Duvose to his feet, keeping the man turned away from him.

"I'm the law here now," Zeke said to the back of Duvose's head, but his voice was loud enough to carry through the restaurant. "Man beats up on a woman, you bring it to me. Man steals your cattle, you bring it to me.

We're done settling grudges with guns in this town. If I see a man walking the streets armed, I'm taking his guns and putting him in the jail. That's all there is to it."

Zeke pushed Duvose toward the door. "Go on home. Look after your sister. Come by the marshal's office tomorrow and you can get your gun back."

Josh Becker likewise pushed MacIntosh toward the door. "Go on home, Shorty," Becker said.

A couple of the men in the restaurant took O'Malley to the hotel across the street and someone summoned the town doctor. The bullet passed through O'Malley's side and out his back before it hit his spine. He was stung, no doubt, but O'Malley would recover from the wound.

***

For four days Sorrel Creek was quiet and peaceful as any town in Vermont. Folks were neighborly, tipping their hats and saying howdy as they passed on the street. Word spread fast that the new town marshal had been on the job for just a couple of hours and he'd already pistol-whipped Carlos Santos and shot down Paddy O'Malley.

It didn't hurt none, either, that the former marshal Josh Becker, a man who was still known and respected in town, was backing up the new marshal.

Carson wasn't too pleased that the shooting took place in his restaurant, but when he saw that men were going around town without their guns, he'd conceded that shooting Paddy O'Malley had been a good thing.

Even the drunks were friendlier.

Zeke ended up keeping the former deputy marshal

employed. He checked in the guns that folks brought by the marshal's office to stow while they were in town. Meanwhile, Zeke and Josh Becker typically positioned themselves in rocking chairs on the plank sidewalks in the center of town, one on one side of the street and the other opposite him.

Being on opposite sides of the street gave them a good vantage to prevent anyone from sneaking up on them. Being in the center of town allowed them to be close if something happened anywhere in town. And being on the street like that allowed them to watch for anyone who was armed.

When they encountered an armed man, they sent him to the marshal's office to check his gun. If he declined, they instructed that man to leave town. Only once did a man flat refuse, and Zeke beat the man into the dirt road, disarmed him and sent him home.

Carlos Santos and Paddy O'Malley continued to occupy cells in the jail. Zeke decided both men could use some time in the town jail to reform. The county judge, like the sheriff, had never made an appearance in Sorrel Creek, and when the last municipal judge was shot and killed, no one else was willing to accept an appointment. So Zeke found himself in the not unusual position of being both the enforcement and judicial arm of the law in a frontier town.

O'Malley, still recuperating from his wound, never did complain. But Santos complained loudly most all the time. Sometimes he begged and other times he threatened, but Carlos Santos was known around town as a rough man, and his presence in the jail was helping to keep everyone else acting respectably.

For Zeke, the most pleasant part of his job came in

the mornings when Annie Becker came to the marshal's office. Josh Becker's wife and daughter cooked breakfast for the marshal and any inmates in the jail every morning. They'd done it since Becker was the marshal, and when he quit the job they continued to do it. The town paid them a fee for the service.

Annie Becker smelled like cooked apples and brown sugar. Zeke was coming up on thirty years old, and Annie was almost ten years younger than him. If she didn't have a daddy who used to be a town marshal and if she wasn't living in one of the roughest towns in Texas, she'd have probably already been married. But there wasn't a man in Sorrel Creek fit to have her, at least not as far as her daddy was concerned.

Her blue eyes and pink complexion, made Zeke's heart beat a little faster when she came through the door, and she had the prettiest sing-song voice he'd ever heard. Mornings were a joy to him. The fact that her blonde hair was as pretty as Sandy's made Zeke feel a special fondness for her.

"Daddy says you have very quickly made some vast improvements to our town, and he's hopeful they will stick," Annie told Zeke on the fourth morning as she took food from a basket. "Why, just yesterday Daddy allowed me to come into town unescorted to buy sugar and apples."

"Is there an apple pie in that basket?" Zeke asked, peering over the top. "I thought I smelled sugar and apples."

Annie Becker ignored his question. "I'm right pleased with the way things are in town now."

"You said Josh wouldn't let you come to town without an escort before? Was it so dangerous a woman couldn't come to town alone?"

Annie unwrapped from a cloth several pieces of bacon and put them on a plate with a biscuit while her mother made coffee at the stove in the office.

"During the daytime it was usually safe enough. It wasn't until evening when the men started to drink heavily. But even during the day, you never knew when two men, both of them holding a grudge against each other, might encounter each other on the street. It was not unheard of that there would be a shooting during the day."

Carlos Santos and Paddy O'Malley were both well behaved when the women were in the office serving breakfast, and Zeke let them out of their cells to eat.

"Of course, Daddy, being a lawman, was always a bit protective," Annie said.

"I'm sure," Zeke said. He could easily imagine it, with Josh Becker's temperament, that he'd watch out for his daughter. Becker also had two sons, near in age to Annie. The older boy lived with his wife just below Sorrel Creek and had a herd of cattle, but the younger boy was still at home. Zeke had only seen the boys a couple of times when they came into town for supplies. Becker didn't much care for any of his children to come to town much, even though they were now all grown.

When the Becker women were gone, Zeke went out to sit on the plank sidewalk. Becker usually didn't come to town until late in the afternoon as he had to see to his mill during the day. But Zeke made himself known on the street, visited the businesses, and sometimes saddled Sandy and rode around town.

Zeke had not forgotten what first brought him to Sorrel Creek, but he did not yet make any effort to ride out to the Chandler homestead.

71

Before leaving Sherman to ride to Sorrel Creek in search of Billy Chandler, Zeke had sent word to his deputy marshals, Jack Bell and the Chickasaw Indian Minko. From all Zeke had heard about the Chandlers, he counted on there being trouble, and he wanted Jack and Minko backing him up.

It took Zeke three days to ride out to Sorrel Creek, and he'd now been here four days. He would have thought Jack and Minko would be along a day or two behind him. There was always the fear, this far out on the plains, that they could have encountered a band of Comanche warriors, but when folks rode into town from the east, no one carried any news of an Indian attack.

Eventually, Zeke knew, he was going to have to deal with Billy Chandler, and he hoped he would not have to do it alone.

***

Early in the afternoon of his fourth day in town, Zeke was leaned back in a chair in front of Wilson's Supply Store. Everything was quiet, and with a spring breeze blowing down the middle of town, Zeke was dozing off a little bit.

Folks were going about their business, walking the street and the plank sidewalk, and Zeke was pretty pleased at the way the town was cleaned up. Buffalo runners and cowpunchers were all behaving themselves. Ranchers felt safe walking their wives and daughters through town.

In the evening, when the sun went down and the cowpunchers and buffalo runners were feeling good from strong drink, it was still not the sort of place a man would want to have his wife walking around by herself, but as far as Zeke could determine, everyone was abiding by the law and leaving their guns at home. The result was a few drunken fistfights in the evenings, but no killings.

Zeke heard the man's footfalls stop in front of him on the plank sidewalk, and the new town marshal opened his eyes and looked out from below the brim of his hat. Zeke's hand had already slid down to the six shooter on his hip.

"Amazing what happens to a place when they's a lawman about who don't mind beating a drunk in the street or shooting a man in a restaurant," the man said.

Zeke looked first for a gun, but the holster on the man's hip was empty.

"I checked my gun, Marshal, if that's what you're looking for."

The man was tall and strong-built. He looked to be about thirty years old, close to Zeke's age. He wore decent trousers and coat of black, with a black and white checkered shirt and a black hat.

"I don't reckon we've met," Zeke said.

"Name is Clive Chandler."

"You one of the Chandlers that shot the last marshal, Marshal Roberts?" Zeke asked.

"I was not," Clive said. "That was some of my cousins."

"Well, they're going to have to come talk to me before long," Zeke said. "I reckon your cousins are going to have to see a judge about shooting the town marshal."

"I'm told you're a marshal for the United States government, too," Clive said.

"I am."

"I understand you've got a warrant for Billy."

"You're getting your information from a good source, Clive," Zeke said. "I am a United States Marshal, and I do have a warrant for Billy Chandler. He shot and killed two United States Deputy Marshals, and he's going to have to see a federal judge over that."

Clive spit tobacco juice between Zeke's feet.

"You want to clean up this town, that's all right by me. It was getting to rough anyway. Not safe for a man to wet his whistle. But you ain't going to take my brother so he can be hanged. Now I've told Billy to stay out of town for a bit. My cousins, too. You won't see none of them around. But if you come out to our place, I'll give you fair warning, Marshal Roberts won't be the last Sorrel Creek marshal the Chandlers kill."

Zeke cracked a smile. He could not help but wonder how his deputy Jack Bell would handle Clive Chandler. Jack's temper could run pretty hot, and he wasn't likely to tolerate a man like Clive Chandler talking to him in such a manner.

"What you smilin' about Marshal?"

Zeke sighed heavily and pushed his hat back on his head so he could see Clive proper. Then he stood up, keeping his hand on the grip of his Colt.

"Clive, easiest thing would be for you to have your brother Billy ride on into town. Might as well send the cousins that shot Marshal Roberts, too. Send 'em on to the marshal's office, and if I ain't there, tell 'em to wait on me.

That's the easiest way. Otherwise, I'm going to have to put together a posse and ride on out to your place, and you and I both know that won't be good for nobody."

"I've said my peace," Clive Chandler said. "You think on it, Marshal, and decide how you want to play it."

Late that evening, when the decent folks were all at home and the rough men were drinking in the saloons, Al Stevens got drunk and started teasing Mikey Epps. Epps was just a boy, not more than sixteen years old, and he felt humiliated by the teasing. Al had boxed his ears and called him a runt, and everyone in the saloon had been laughing.

Mikey, who didn't have no family and was living in a tent outside of town, left the saloon and came back a bit later with a six shooter under his coat. When Al Stevens left the saloon a while later, Mike Epps shot him once in the stomach and once in the chest.

Josh Becker and Zeke Thornton were just a block away. Mikey, who'd never killed a man before, didn't have the sense to run and was still standing over Al Stevens' body when Zeke and Josh got to him.

Zeke bashed the teenage boy across the side of the head with the barrel of his Colt, and Mikey was sprawled out on the ground. They took Mike down to the marshal's office and put him in the empty jail cell.

The shooting was the undoing of the law in Sorrel Creek.

Mikey Epps hadn't been in the jail cell for a half hour before an angry, drunken mob was gathering outside of the marshal's office.

Zeke and Josh Becker met the mob at the plank sidewalk in front of the marshal's office. Zeke had his Henry

PEECHER

rifle in his hands, and Becker was toting the double barrel shotgun he preferred. Both men had Colts holstered.

When Zeke saw that the mob was led by Clive Chandler, he understood that this was about something other than the shooting of Al Stevens.

"Al Stevens was unarmed and murdered in cold blood," Clive Chandler yelled at the marshals. The mob reacted angrily, hollering and demanding Mikey Epps be brought to them.

Clive was smiling at Zeke, clearly he enjoyed this turn of events. Clive waited for the mob to quiet down some, and then he yelled back to them, "If the marshal can't protect us from being shot like dogs, then we should be able to rearm ourselves!"

That stirred the mob into a frenzy.

"If they come for the marshal's office to get that boy, I'm shooting Clive Chandler first," Zeke mumbled to Becker.

"Suits me," Becker said.

"You want to try to reason with them?" Zeke asked. "They know you better than me."

"You're the marshal," Becker said. "I'm just here to back you up."

Zeke spared a glance at Becker, who was grinning at him.

Zeke stepped to the edge of the plank sidewalk, and the mob generally quieted down and turned its attention to the new town marshal.

"Clive, if you don't hush up, I'm going to put you in

76

that jail cell with Mikey Epps for unruly behavior and inciting a mob. Now listen folks, there ain't no doubt that Mikey Epps killed that man tonight, and Mikey is where he belongs. He's in a jail cell waiting for a trial. If y'all will go on home and sleep it off, then in the morning, Mikey will still be in the jail cell and y'all won't be in there with him. So go on home."

Someone from deep in the crowd yelled out, "Al Stevens was a good man!"

Now Josh Becker stepped forward.

"No he warn't!" Becker said. "Al Stevens was a bully and a drunkard and a cow thief, and every man in this town knows it. He probably done worse. I ain't saying that gave Mikey the right to shoot him. Of course it did not, but anyone who stands here and says that Al Stevens didn't deserve shooting is a liar or didn't know Al Stevens."

A couple of people in the crowd laughed, and Zeke thought there seemed to be general agreement.

Clive Chandler gritted his teeth, and Zeke could see his jawbone working.

"Al Stevens might have deserved to get shot," Clive called out, "but that don't mean the rest of us should continue to go about unarmed. Nothing about Al's character changes the fact that he was disarmed by the law and unable to defend hisself when that boy drawed down on him."

A drunken crowd sways easy, and each new compelling argument presented before it seemed to have all the strength and accuracy of the previous argument. So now the crowd was angry again.

Clive took up a chant. "Give us back our guns!" he

hollered and repeated it a couple of times, and soon every man in the mob was chanting along.

But the chants fell to silence with the booming crack of the rifle.

Zeke and Josh Becker both drew up their weapons and looked for the source of the shot, and in a moment two men armed with rifles stepped from the dark shadows away from the mob into the light cast by the torches and the lamp light coming from the windows of the marshal's office.

The men were both tall and strong looking, and Josh Becker immediately sized them up as men who made their way with their guns. One was a handsome, young white fellow. The other looked to be an Indian, maybe a Cherokee, with long black hair and dark features.

With the attention of the mob on him, the white man called out, "I'm a Deputy United States Marshal. If this mob does not disperse posthaste, that man shot outside the saloon tonight ain't going to be the last man killed. Y'all go on home before I shoot you dead. I'll kill every damn one of you."

With the dark Indian fellow pointing a Henry rifle into the mob, this seemed to be the most compelling argument of the evening. The mob immediately broke up with men drifting off in every direction.

Clive Chandler shot a look at Zeke, but he left, too.

"Friends of yours?" Becker asked as the mob drifted away and the two strangers stood their ground staring menacingly at the dispersing crowd.

Zeke nodded. "Those are the boys I've been waiting for."

***

Jack and Minko rode into town about sundown and got a room at a hotel. They had dinner and sat in one of the saloons and overheard enough conversations to understand that their friend had taken on new responsibilities as a town marshal since they'd last seen him. They'd also heard about Zeke enforcing the no-guns ordinance of the town. Though wearing their badges, Jack and Minko remained armed throughout the evening.

Their intention had been to spend the night in the hotel and find Zeke in the morning at the marshal's office, but the mob in the street changed their plans.

Now they were sitting with Zeke and Josh inside the marshal's office.

"Well, I don't mind telling you, Zeke, if I was one of those boys in the mob I suppose I'd be a bit miffed, too, if you told me I could not go around armed," Jack said. "An unarmed man ain't nothing but a victim in waiting."

"I don't disagree," Zeke conceded. "I reckon a town where a man can't tote a gun, whether it's for defense or just to shoot snakes and such, is not a town where I would care to live. But the way I see it, if I didn't disarm this town and get a hold to some of these folks, one of them was eventually going to shoot me."

"How long are you planning on staying here and being the town marshal?" Minko asked.

Zeke looked at Josh Becker, who was likewise interested in the answer.

"I don't know," Zeke said. "It ain't a permanent

position. I figure I can help get this place cleaned up in a couple of weeks, get it settled down some, and then the aldermen can hire a new marshal who won't have quite as big a job on his hands."

Zeke was still looking at Becker.

"What?" Becker asked. "Me? I ain't going to be the town marshal again."

Zeke shrugged. "If I can make the job safe enough, somebody'll do it."

"What about that warrant that brought you out here?" Bell asked.

"Billy Chandler," Zeke said. "That was his older brother leading the mob out there. We may have a time serving that warrant. They've got a place about twenty miles west of town. I haven't been out there to scout it, yet, but it seems likely they'll meet our warrant with pistols."

"Point me in the right direction, and in the morning me and Minko will ride out there and scout the place."

***

The Chandlers had built their homes in a hollow down by a creek. The houses were surrounded by some cottonwoods and a few big hardwood trees. Jack and Minko rode their horses north of the homestead and followed the creek down close to the houses.

They weren't much. A couple of log cabins, roughly built, that leaked any breeze that blew, cold or warm. The homes served as a place to bed down and not much more. But there were some womenfolk who all looked to be of Mexican blood. The boys had made a half-hearted attempt at doing some farming, and there was a small vegetable crop. They had some cows nearby, and Jack guessed those cows were of various brands. The finest structure on the site was the stable, and there were numerous horses grazing in the grass in a corral not far from the place.

Bell and Minko recognized Clive when he walked to the outhouse. They counted four other men milling about the place, but there could have been others inside. They all seemed to be doing a fair amount of loafing and not much else. Nothing that Jack or Minko witnessed looked anything like work.

Other than coming along the creek through the cottonwoods, as Jack and Minko had done, there didn't appear to be a good way to sneak up on the cabin. It was down in a bit of a hollow, and a rider out on the plains would not be seen coming from town unless one of the Chandler boys was standing up on the high ground. But if someone was standing up on the high ground, he wouldn't have to be looking to see a rider coming along through the tall grass. And a posse would be visible from more than a mile away.

"Only way in here without being seen is along the creek," Minko whispered to Jack.

"I think that's right."

"But we can't get any closer than this coming in along the creek," Minko said.

Currently, Jack and Minko were within a hundred yards of the first house.

It looked like the boys had cleared some of the cottonwoods out this far. Probably just cutting them for firewood, but the effect was they had cleared a pretty good stretch of ground that would make it impossible for anyone to sneak right up on the houses.

Jack thought out loud. "Maybe get here around dusk, then sneak up to the house after dark. Take them at first light when they're still asleep."

"That would be my thinking on it," Minko agreed.

As they were whispering, they saw Clive Chandler come out of one of the houses. He called to the other men who were out, and they all walked into one of the houses together.

"Wonder what that's about," Minko said.

"Don't know. I doubt they'd have seen us, but you be ready just in case."

Jack and Minko held their position for a long while. Two women were down at the creek washing clothes. Another woman was picking through the vegetable patch, maybe pulling weeds but it was hard to see exactly what she was doing. The men stayed in the far house.

After about three-quarters of an hour, several men came out of the house. There were six of them, including Clive Chandler. Bell tried to pick out which one might be Billy, but it was impossible to say. All of the men were carrying rifles and had six-shooters on their hips.

Bell bit his lip and watched them.

"Keep an eye on 'em," he whispered to Minko. "If any of them look like they're trying to flank us, we'll have to stop them."

But the men walked out toward the corral, and each man picked out a horse. They led the horses back to the stable where they saddled them, and in several minutes the men were all mounted and riding out east away from the homestead.

Now a seventh man emerged from one of the houses. Like the others, he walked out to the corral, but he brought back a couple of mules and went to hitching them to a wagon. And now a couple of women were carrying items out of one of the houses and stowing them in the wagon.

"If they know we're here, they might go up out of the holler, and once behind that hill they might try to come in around behind us. We need to get eyes on them, fast," Jack said.

"I never thought they saw us," Minko said.

"All the same, we need to know they ain't coming around behind us. They were in that house for a long time making a plan."

Minko and Jack slowly and quietly backed out of where they were perched to where they'd tied up their horses. Then they led the horses back along the creek through the cover of the cottonwoods, and when they'd gone several hundred yards and thought they'd be out of sight from the hollow, they emerged from the brush and mounted up.

"There they go," Minko said. He'd spotted them out across the grass plain, riding in a southeasterly direction away from the hollow.

"What do you suspect they're up to?" Bell said.

"We didn't see 'em do a bit of honest work around their house all morning. That sort of idleness suggests to me they must have some dishonest work they do. My guess is they're going to work now," Minko said.

"That would be my guess, too."

***

Clive Chandler made his decision when the two Deputy U.S. Marshals showed up to help quell the crowd. If he was going to keep his brothers and his cousins out of the hangman's noose, he was going to have to do it away from Sorrel Creek. But to start over somewhere new, they were going to need money. And the wealthiest man that Clive Chandler knew was the man who owned the gristmill in Sorrel Creek.

Josh Becker had his hand in everything. He had an interest in one of the supply stores. He had a big herd of cattle. He owned the gristmill. And he also owned one of the saloons. Back when Josh Becker was still the town marshal, folks used to joke that he got sober men drunk and then arrested the drunk men so he could sober them up in his jail and then turn them loose so they could go get drunk again.

Clive didn't like the notion of messing with women. It went against the way he was raised. But as they kicked around ideas for how to part Josh Becker from his cash, the boys all agreed the simplest way would be to take Annie Becker and give her back for five hundred dollars in gold and silver coins. Everyone in town knew Becker kept that kind of money.

Snatching Annie Becker from her home would be a simple enough task. Josh Becker was back to being a lawman, so he wouldn't be around the house in the early evening. Especially not after the trouble from the night before.

Even outlaws tended to respect decent women, but Clive was feeling desperate. He didn't like the look of the new town marshal, and he didn't like the look of the deputy federal marshals, neither. He knew, too, that the deputies were in town for his brother.

So he left his brother Billy at the homestead with the women to load all the valuables into the two buckboard wagons. The women could drive them wagons out onto the plain a ways, and Billy could herd a couple dozen cows. The rest of the boys would go and get the girl, and Clive would send the mama to find Josh Becker and tell him if he wanted his daughter back it was going to cost him five hundred dollars in gold and silver coins.

Even though he didn't like it, the boys convinced Clive this was the best way to get at Becker's money, and now Clive Chandler was convincing himself it was a good plan.

***

"I think your sweet on Marshal Thornton."

Annie Becker blushed. "Mama, don't say such a thing."

The two Becker women were standing in the kitchen at the stove making preserves with the first blackberries of spring.

"I seen you put two pieces of ham on his plate this morning," Mrs. Becker teased her daughter.

"Oh, Mama. Just stop that."

"Well, you know he's sweet on you," her mother said. "I can tell by the way he looks at you. But I'll tell you this, a woman who marries a lawman spends a lot of time awake and lonely in the middle of the night."

Annie Becker stamped her foot. "Mama, nobody is talking about getting married."

"That, my sweet girl, is simply not so. Somebody is talking about getting married."

"Who?" Annie asked.

"Marshal Thornton was asking your daddy yesterday afternoon if there was any man you took an interest in."

Annie rolled her eyes. "You're teasing me, Mama. That ain't marriage talk."

"That ain't all he said."

"What else did he say?" Annie asked, hoping her voice didn't betray how interested she was.

"Your daddy asked Marshal Thornton if he was looking for a dancing partner for Friday evening's dance or if he was looking for a wife. And Marshal Thornton said a man could do worse than having Annie Becker for a wife."

"That's not what he said."

"It is," Mrs. Becker insisted. "That's exactly what he told your pa. I'd say he's sweet on you."

Annie turned at a noise and in her surprise at seeing the man standing in her home, she dropped the glass jar full of preserves. It broke on the floor. But Annie quickly composed herself. "Clive Chandler, what are you doing in my house?" she demanded.

***

"They ain't taking grain to the mill," Minko said.

The deputy federal marshals followed the Chandler gang out across the plains all the way back to Sorrel Creek.

Bell and Minko rode back and followed the dust trail the boys left, but the Chandlers never once checked their back trail to be sure they weren't followed. The boys crossed the river at a ford well south of town. Bell and Minko let them get ahead and then crossed behind them.

Down here by the river there were hardwoods down in the river valley, and Minko and Bell rode down among the hardwoods while the Chandler boys were up on the road. When they neared the gristmill just south of town, the Chandler boys dismounted and walked their horses down in among the hardwoods and into the undergrowth near the riverbank. One of the Chandlers stood with the horses while the others walked toward the gristmill.

The deputy marshals held their horses down among the stand of trees and waited.

"What do you think?" Bell asked.

"I don't know what to think," Minko admitted.

"Damn odd behavior for a bunch of outlaws with no grain to visit a gristmill like this."

"We could jump the boy they left with the horses," Minko suggested. "Make him tell us what they're doing."

"To my knowledge, that boy hasn't broken a law. Unless it's Billy Chandler, we ain't got no legal reason to jump him."

Minko shrugged. Before becoming a Confederate

officer, Jack Bell had studied the law some with a thought to becoming a lawyer. He often talked about what was legal and what was not. All Minko knew was that they had followed a gang of outlaws who appeared to be up to no good, and now one of them was alone and would be easy enough to grab.

Several minutes passed, and there was nothing to indicate what the Chandler boys were up to. Whoever owned the gristmill had his house there nearby the mill, and Bell wondered if maybe the Chandler boys had gone to see the owner of the mill and had not gone to the mill at all.

"Maybe they know somebody who works at the mill and they're just paying a visit," Jack said, shifting in his saddle.

"Maybe."

Minko leaned forward in his saddle as if to get a better look.

"We're about to know something in a minute, Jack. They're coming back now, and it looks like they're in a hurry."

"Is that a girl they've got with them?" Bell asked.

"Sure is. And she don't look none too happy about it."

One of the Chandler boys, it looked like Clive, had a girl tossed over his shoulder like a sack of potatoes, and she was kicking up a storm.

It took a couple of the Chandler boys to hold her still and get her over Clive's saddle. Bell couldn't say for sure, but the way she was holding her arms together, it sure looked like her wrists were tied.

"Are they kidnapping that girl?" Minko asked.

"Looks that away," Jack said. "You think you could hit a couple of them with your Henry from this distance without any risk of hitting the girl?"

The Chandler boys were all mounting, now, and they were starting to wheel their horses back toward the road. In a moment, they'd be galloping past where Jack and Minko sat.

"I could hit a couple of them, but I can't guarantee I could shoot Clive without hitting the girl. Especially now that they're on the move."

"Yep. Me neither."

The deputy marshals watched the Chandler boys ride like thunder down the road. None of them ever saw Jack and Minko sitting their horses down among the trees.

"What do we do?" Minko asked.

"You ride into town and get Zeke. Tell him what we've seen. Tell him to get together a posse. I'll follow these boys and leave a good trail for you."

Bell drew out his Bowie knife and rode his cavalry horse, Petey, over to some branches with fresh green leaves. He skinned a couple of branches, shoving the twigs with the green leaves down into his saddlebags.

If this was in fact a kidnapping, the Chandlers would be watching their back trail now, and Jack didn't want to get too close behind them.

***

It was not far beyond the river when the landscape

opened up to open plain with rolling hills. The Chandlers were riding hard, and as such they kicked up enough dust that it was easy to follow them from a distance. Bell, as a lone rider, wouldn't kick up so much dust. As long as he stayed out of sight, he wasn't worried that they would know they were being followed.

They started west across the plains, riding back toward their homes, but when they came to a worn buffalo trace, they cut south. Here, Bell dismounted and pulled some of the twigs with green leaves from his saddle bag. He dug a little hole with his Bowie knife in the hard ground and stuck the twig in the hole so that the green leaves would be pointing up. Then he used the heel of his boot to scratch an arrow pointing south into the dirt.

He rode another twenty yards and then dropped a couple of twigs with green leaves onto the ground, one more hint to make sure Minko and Zeke knew which way to go. The green leaves proved to serve as an adequate beacon against the brown grass and dirt.

It wouldn't be more than a couple of hours of daylight. If the Chandlers rode on past nightfall they would be harder to follow. And even with Jack leaving a trail, Minko and Zeke and the posse would have a hard time following.

Bell hoped the Chandler boys weren't planning to take this girl too far.

He puzzled over what they might have wanted with her. Maybe one of the boys was sweet on her and figured he could abduct her and convince her to marry him. Like most other things out on the frontier, courting was often done differently than it might be done back east.

Maybe they hoped to sell her to the Comanche,

though if the Comanche wanted a white girl they had their own way of getting one.

Bell had some concerns that the Chandlers had some trouble with the man who owned the gristmill, and they'd taken the girl to get revenge over something. It was a hard man that would kill a woman to get back at her pa, but Bell knew that the Chandlers had killed at least three lawmen. Even so, most outlaws wouldn't go after a woman to get back at a man.

He wondered about the girl. Was she the gristmill owner's wife? She looked mighty young, but not so young that she couldn't be married. More likely his daughter.

Bell was probably ten minutes behind the Chandlers when they veered off of the buffalo trace to go back west.

He dropped out of the saddle and repeated leaving a mark with the green leaves. Now he was just riding out across open range, and Bell dropped twigs frequently. He was worried he might run out, but if there was any hope of saving the girl, Bell was going to need help doing it. He had to do what he could to make certain the posse could find him.

After riding for another half hour or so, the dust trail Jack had been following settled down.

Bell staked Petey to the ground at the base of a hill, and then he walked to the top to see if he had any vantage that would allow him to see the Chandlers. He took his field glasses with him.

About two miles off in the distance, Bell could see a small outcropping of rock, an odd sight out here on the plains. Odder still, the women and the one man who'd stayed behind at the Chandler place were here with two covered wagons. Several head of cattle were here, too. A sheet of canvas was strung up as protection from the sun, and the Chandlers had all dismounted. They put the girl in a chair under the sheet of canvas. As best as he could tell, she was not coming to any harm.

Bell watched them. He decided if they made to take advantage of her, he would ride into their camp with the rifle spitting fire and do what he could to get her away.

Bell made his way back down the hill without making any movements that might get him discovered. He drank a little water from his canteen and got a couple of strips of jerky for supper. It would be dark soon. He gave Petey some water and then made his way back up the hill to take another look at the camp. Nothing much had changed. The men were lazing about. The women were cooking over a small fire. The kidnapped girl was still sitting under the canvas.

Bell checked his back trail. There was no sign of a posse.

**

Bell woke with a start and immediately grabbed hold of his Henry rifle.

He hated waking up on the ground. For the better part of four years, Jack Bell woke up on the ground, and now that the war was over he preferred a bed.

The blue light of dawn glowed in the sky, but the earth was still black as night. Bell looked around to see if he could determine what had awakened him. Petey was standing asleep.

Bell stretched and pushed himself up off the ground. He walked back up to the top of the hill. It was still too dark to see anything, but a few minutes more and there would be light enough to see into the camp.

Down below him, Petey snorted. Bell let his eyes adjust. He could see a shadow coming from the camp. Someone was running and was getting very near to him. The movement was odd, the way someone might run if their hands were bound in front of them.

As she neared, Bell could discern that it was the kidnapped girl. She would pass a hundred yards west of the hill where Jack was perched, and he suspected that in the dark she would not see Petey.

Bell took a long, slow look down the trail from where the girl was running back to the camp. He could make out no movements behind her. The Chandlers did not know the girl was running. But as he peered through his field glasses at the camp, he saw a lantern light begin to glow. They would know in a few moments.

Bell didn't hesitate. He didn't have time to devise a plan.

He scrambled down the hill and ran the distance to intercept the girl. As she neared him, she was breathing hard and stumbling, and she didn't see him in the dark. As she came within reach, Bell grabbed her up, put a hand over her mouth, and pulled her tight into him.

"I'm a deputy marshal," Bell said to the girl. "I'm going to protect you. Everything is going to be okay. I'm going to take my hand off your mouth, but don't scream or talk too loud. They're awake back at the camp and they know by now that you've gotten away."

The girl, still breathing hard and gasping for breath around Jack's hand, nodded a panicked nod. Jack let loose of her mouth.

"Everything's going to be okay," Bell repeated. "Come with me now."

Bell led the girl at a fast pace back to the hill.

"You stay here with my horse. If something happens and they get me, you just ride hard to the east. A posse is coming this way. Petey here used to be in the Yankee cavalry. He can outrun any mount they have. So even if something happens to me, you'll still be able to get away."

The girl nodded, still trying to catch her breath.

Now Bell hurried back up the hill. He didn't worry about making any movements. No one from the camp would see him yet.

They were walking around the camp, several of them holding lanterns and looking around. Through the field glasses, Bell could see them arguing.

He'd been a lawman long enough that he always did enjoy watching outlaws when they realized their plan had gone awry. They'd grumble and complain and blame each other and cuss a bit, and it was at that moment – as accusations were being passed back and forth among the gang – that they were always at their weakest. If the Chandlers hadn't all been related, Bell might have expected one or two of them to go for their guns.

Now a couple of them were saddling up their horses. They were planning to give chase, try to catch the girl.

A noise behind him made Jack turn around. The girl

was coming up the hill.

"Stay down low," Bell hissed at her. "It's getting light quick. I can't have them know we're here."

"They'll come for me," the girl said.

"I'm counting on it," Bell told her. "Who are you?"

"I'm Annie Becker," the girl said. "My daddy is Josh Becker, a deputy marshal in Sorrel Creek."

"What did they want with you?" Bell asked.

"They come into our house yesterday and took me, and they told my mama to go and find my daddy and tell him that if he wanted to see me alive again he was going to have to pay them five hundred dollars. They said they'd bring me at noon today to Two Springs Creek and that my mama should bring them the money in a wagon today."

Bell hoped that Zeke and Minko were bringing a posse here and not headed off to Two Springs Creek.

"How far is Two Springs Creek from here?"

"I don't know where we are," Annie Becker said. "I couldn't say how far it is."

Bell was watching the camp through the field glasses.

"Here they come. Go on back down to my horse. But don't ride off unless I'm shot. The only way I can hold them off is if you're right here with me. You promise me you can keep cool?"

"I can."

"Don't panic. Just stay there with my horse."

The riders were coming on hard, closing the

distance in a hurry. Jack Bell flipped up the ladder sight on his Henry rifle and kept it trained on one of the men riding at him. He knew as soon as he pulled the trigger things would get hot in a jiffy.

The crack of the rifle seemed to break the quiet from one end of the Texas plain to the other. One of the two riders coming toward him dropped from the saddle and fell into the tall grass. The other reined in and jumped from his horse, rushing to the fallen rider. Bell thought it was Clive Chandler he shot, but he couldn't be sure at this distance without the field glasses.

These two riders were back tracking the way they'd come, and they had been coming fast. Four other men were mounted back at the camp and were riding short distances in various directions looking for signs of the girl. But with the rifle shot, all of the other mounted men had turned their horses and were coming in this direction.

The second rider, the one Bell did not shoot, stood up and looked across the plain, obviously trying to see who had shot his buddy.

The man made his way to his horse and drew out a rifle from its scabbard. He was still looking. He still didn't know where the shot had come from.

Bell took aim and fired again. His second shot hit the man in the arm, spun him and knocked him down. Both men were now out of the fight.

The four riders reined in and stopped their advance.

This was a gang of outlaws that was having a bad start to the day. They'd lost the girl they had kidnapped and were holding for ransom. Two of their number had been shot. And they did not know where the shots had come from.

Bell picked up the field glasses. Everything at the camp was chaos. The women were arguing with each other and one of them was trying to pull away from the others. The four mounted men were also arguing with each other. They were beyond his range, but Bell considered firing another shot anyway. He liked the idea of the rifle crack sounding across the plain, and he hoped it would spur the posse to come on a bit quicker.

He looked over his shoulder to check on the girl, and he was pleased to see she was standing firm by the horse.

The wounded man was struggling to mount his horse. The other man had not moved from the tall grass. Bell figured that man was dead or nearly so.

The wounded man managed his saddle and galloped hard back toward the others. He reined in there and conferred with them, and then he rode back toward the camp. The way he rode, leaning and with one arm drooping at his side, Bell could see that he'd hurt the man bad.

They had too much ground to cover to get at Bell, even if they knew where he was. He could shoot all four of them before they ever reached him. If they tried to split their numbers and flank him, Bell would still have plenty of time to gun them down. They didn't have numbers enough to overwhelm him.

Other than the wounded man, there was still one man back at the camp. Through the field glasses, Bell could see that this man had made no effort to join the others. Instead, he was hitching up the mules and breaking down the camp. When the wounded man arrived back to camp, the womenfolk all huddled around him and began bandaging his wound.

Bell wondered what the four mounted men were debating. They were probably trying to decide whether to make a run for it or to stand and fight. Now one of the four turned and rode back to camp, but the other three sat their horses where they were.

Jack Bell could lay there in that tall grass all day if he had to, but he didn't care for the waiting. He'd prefer to get on with it.

The rider who'd gone back to camp was now making his way back out to the other three, and the group of them held another parley.

***

"I'm telling you, we ain't missing a rifle," Billy Chandler told his brother Went. "I checked, and there ain't none missing. Besides, that girl couldn't have shot Clive and Jeffrey like that. Annie Becker ain't no sharpshooter. Someone else is out there."

With Clive shot through the chest and laying dead in the grass, Went figured, as the next to oldest, he was now in charge of the Chandler gang. It was Clive and Cousin Jeffrey who rode out after the girl and both got shot. Cousin Jeffrey was shot through the shoulder, and his Mexican wife and the other women were seeing to him. Went Chandler rubbed his chin and looked out across the tall grass.

"Ain't nobody tracked us in the dark, and nobody followed us out of town. How could they know where we's at?" Went wasn't really asking anybody. He was just thinking out loud.

Besides Billy, there were the cousins Gilmer and Ward mounted out here with Went and Billy. Cousin Jeffrey was back at camp, wounded, and Cousin Frank was packing up the gear and breaking down the camp so they could ride on if they had to abandon the plan. And it was looking increasingly like they were going to have to abandon the plan.

"It's almost got to be the girl," Went said. "She snuck a rifle and she's trying to hold us off."

Billy shook his head in disgust. "It's probably a whole damn posse, and they're probably circling around us right now."

Went's mind was on that five hundred dollars. He hated to not get it. If they let the girl go, the money was gone.

"We can't just leave Clive out there," Gilmer offered. "What if Jeffrey's wrong and he's still alive?"

Went spat tobacco juice into the dust. "Well, ride on out there, Gilmer, and check on him."

Gilmer started to turn his horse, but Billy grabbed the tackle and pulled the horse's head back around. "He ain't serious, Gilmer," Billy said. "You ride out there, you'll get shot, too."

But that gave Went an idea.

"You're the best horseman, Billy. You ride out there."

"I ain't riding out there," Billy said.

"You ride hard out that way some and then come on back. We'll watch and we'll see where she's shooting from."

Billy shook his head and rolled his eyes. "Went, I'm telling you, that ain't her out there shooting. There ain't no way a'tall that girl shot Clive in the chest with one shot and got Jeffrey in the arm with the second shot. There's a posse out yonder, and they'll gun down any man who tempts 'em."

Went spat into the ground again. He drew his rifle out of its scabbard and handed it to Billy. "Hold this," he said. Then he pulled his revolver from its holster and gave that to Gilmer. "You hold this. I've got an idea."

Went didn't have any kind of white flag, but he undid his red bandana and held it over his head in one hand. Then he urged his horse into a walk and started out on his own toward his dead brother.

The whole time, Went's eyes scanned the horizon looking for any sign of a man or a woman, but he saw nothing.

The low hill in front of him seemed to be the most likely spot. It was the only real vantage point anywhere near where the shot would have come from. Went kept his eyes on that hill.

When he got near to where Clive's horse was standing, Went called out as loud as he could, "I'm going to check on my brother. He's hurt real bad. I ain't armed, so don't shoot me."

He hoped there would be a reply, but there was not.

Went got up level with Clive's horse and he dismounted. As he did, he noticed Clive's rifle in its scabbard. That gave him a new idea.

Went walked over to Clive and kneeled down

beside him. "Dammit, Clive. You're deader than a door nail."

He stood back up. "You killed my brother!" Went yelled at the hilltop in front of him.

There was still no reply, but with the morning sun well up now, Went saw what he was looking for. The polished brass of the receiver of a Henry rifle was gleaming through the grass on top of the hill. And following it, Went could see the shape of a man lying prone behind it.

"Who are you?" Went yelled. Again, there was no answer. "Dammit! I'm talking to ye!"

Went spit tobacco juice in frustration, and he felt a twinge of guilt when he realized he'd spit it ride on Clive's face.

The silence coming from the man on the hilltop and the fact that he'd just spit into his dead brother's face had Went Chandler all kinds of riled now.

Went walked back to his horse and stepped into the stirrup. As he did, the horse moved toward Clive's horse. Now Went moved fast. He swung his leg over the saddle, leaned far over to grab Clive's rifle, and now he wheeled his horse toward the hilltop and pushed it forward at a hard gallop. The distance was closing fast. Went fired a shot, cocked the gun and let loose another shot. There was no return fire from the hilltop, and that puzzled Went. How could a man just lay there with another man charging down on him? Went cocked the rifle and fired again. A hundred yards turned into fifty, and Went fired a fourth shot with Clive's rifle. Then he saw the puff of smoke on the hilltop, and in that same second he felt the bullet punch him in the gut.

"Ah hell!" Went yelled as he fell from the saddle.

"Oh, damn! I'm gut shot boys! Oh, damn!"

Went was squirming like the devil, and his stomach was on fire. He didn't know where his horse had got to, but he didn't care. Went Chandler knew he was dying. He never did let go of the rifle, not even when he hit the ground so hard. Went pushed himself up off the ground and cocked the rifle. He fired another shot at the hilltop. He could not believe he'd not hit the man there. Now he was walking toward the hill. He fired another shot. But it was getting hard to walk because his legs felt so heavy. He fired another shot, but this one just spit out at the sky. He tried to level the rifle at the hilltop again, but that's when Went Chandler realized he was on his back. He pulled the trigger anyway and sent another lead ball skyward. Then he dropped Clive's rifle.

When Billy Chandler watched his brother fall into the grass, it took him a moment to realize that he was now the last of his brothers still alive. He intended to remain so. Billy didn't say anything to Gilmer or Ward. He spun his horse and gave him spurs and raced off to the south. Billy Chandler was on the dodge, and he was going alone.

Far beyond the hill where Went had been shooting, Gilmer and Ward saw the dust kicking up.

"They's riders coming fast," Ward said.

"That's got to be a posse," Gilmer said.

"We'd best go with Billy," Ward suggested.

Billy did not see the dust trail, and when Gilmer and Ward got to camp, they didn't bother to say anything to him about it right away. If he'd known a dust trail was coming at them hard, Billy would have ridden on out of there. But he stopped at the camp to get provisions. He filled two canteens. He got some jerky.

"I'm riding back to Dallas," Billy told his cousins. "Y'all spread out in different directions. Let the women take the wagons. Make your way to Dallas, and meet me there."

"How are we going to lose the posse?" Gilmer asked.

"They ain't coming yet," Billy said.

"Sure they is," Gilmer said. "We saw the dust trail."

Billy looked behind him in time to see a dozen riders rapidly closing the distance on the camp.

"Oh, hell!" Billy said, and without grabbing any more previsions, he jumped into his saddle and started to ride.

If Gilmer or Ward or Frank had given thought to further flight, they missed their chance. The posse was in among them, pointing rifles down at them.

Two men in the posse were charging hard after Billy, and one of them on a pretty chestnut with a blonde mane had let loose his reins and was drawing down on Billy with a Henry rifle.

The rifle cracked, and the cousins watched as Billy Chandler fell from his saddle.

Zeke Thornton had served the warrant that brought him to Sorrel Creek.

***

The wound Jack Bell took was his own fault. When he shot Went Chandler off the horse, Bell knew it was a mortal shot. Went got back up and started shooting at the hilltop, and Bell thought about dropping him with another shot but figured he'd already done the damage and didn't need to fire again. But one of Went's last shots, before he fell on his back and started shooting at the sky, had hit a rock not two feet from Jack's face, and a chip of rock flung up and hit him in the cheekbone. He was bleeding like hell, but it only stung a little bit.

The posse was already riding at a good pace when they heard the shooting. Several rapid shots. It was Went Chandler making his final assault on the hilltop that they heard. They came on hard when they heard the shots.

Zeke Thornton was surprised at the relief he felt when he saw Annie Becker standing beside Petey. He'd taken a liking to her in the few days that he'd been in Sorrel Creek, but he'd had a sick feeling in his chest ever since Minko found him and explained about the Chandler boys going into the home by the gristmill and abducting a girl.

Zeke and Josh Becker had been together when Minko told the tale, and both men knew that it was Annie who'd been abducted.

But seeing Annie safe and whole, the sick feeling in Zeke's chest disappeared.

Josh Becker broke away from the rest of the posse when he saw Bell's horse and his daughter standing at the foot of the hill. He rode directly to her and leapt from his horse and threw his arms around her.

When the posse rode past, Bell stood up and walked down the hill where Annie Becker made too much of a fuss over his bleeding cheek.

Zeke and Minko chased after the man who tried to

flee the camp, and when he was close enough to make a sure shot, Zeke shot him out of his saddle with his Henry rifle. Billy Chandler was probably dead before he hit the ground.

The cousins all faced charges of kidnapping the girl, but Zeke also had warrants on three of them for shooting and killing the previous town marshal. It didn't matter none what the charges were. All four of them would hang.

Jack and Minko spent a couple more days in Sorrel Creek to let their horses rest and to rest themselves, but they were both eager to get home.

"I'm going to stay on another month," Zeke told them as they saddled up at the livery and prepared to ride back to Two Rivers Station. "Josh Becker has agreed to serve as town marshal again, but I'm going to stay on as his deputy for a few more weeks and help make sure this place stays quiet. Hanging four men will probably help."

"Is that the only reason you're staying?" Bell asked.

"Maybe not," Zeke confessed.

"Annie Becker's a good cook," Minko said.

"Yes she is," Zeke said.

"If a man were looking for a wife, he could do a great deal worse than getting one who's a good cook," Jack said.

Zeke laughed. "I was thinking along them same lines, too."

THE BUFFALO RUNNER

Minko smelled them before he could see them. Rotting flesh baking in the Texas sun puts off a strong odor.

The Chickasaw man urged his black Morgan horse up the side of the hill to the crest, and from there he could see them spread out on the plain below him. They were like tiny hills of exposed flesh dotting the open grassland. A score of buffalo carcasses rotting in the sun with buzzards picking at the exposed meat.

Minko's tribe was not among those Plains Indians who made their life on the trail of the buffalo. The Comanche, the Lakota, the Kiowa, the Apache – these tribes were as foreign to him as a Chinaman. Minko's Chickasaw people were now two generations in Indian Territory. Minko had more in common with Jack Bell, the Confederate officer from the war who was now Minko's fellow deputy U.S. Marshal, than he had with the Comanche or the Lakota.

Still, Minko did not like the waste. He did not like to see meat that could feed a tribe for a month get pecked at by the birds and devoured by the maggots. There were things about white men that disgusted him, and there were no white men more disgusting than the buffalo runners. Callous and reprehensible killers. The skinners always covered in blood from removing the hides. Most did not even bother to wash before sitting down to supper. And the money they made was all wasted on cheap whiskey not fit for a horse to drink and women whose beds smelled like dead bison.

The men had probably been up on this hill. They'd have seen the buffalo trace below them. Maybe they waited a day or two for the bison to come to them or maybe they came upon the beasts grazing. The buffalo runners had camped on the side of the hill opposite the buffalo trace. Down below there was the remains of a campfire, cold now with nothing but gray ash and the ends of blackened sticks. Whether the buffalo were there when the men arrived, grazing on the tall grass, or whether the men waited a day or two for the buffalo to appear, it didn't make no difference.

The men would have kneeled or perhaps sat on this hilltop, taking aim with their heavy Sharps rifles, the barrels resting on wooden stands. The first crack of the Sharps would have taken down but not killed the matron cow, the leader of the small herd. The dumb beasts did not stampede when their leader was killed. They just milled about, pawing at the wounded cow. And then they fell when hit by the big lead balls from the Sharps.

Bison were beasts meant for killing and not much else. Too dumb and ill equipped to protect themselves. Their only natural defense was to run, but they were too slow to escape a horse or a wolf, and they were too dumb to run if the buffalo runner knew his business.

Wound but do not kill the cow. Without the herd's leader, the buffalo were thrown into a state of paralyzed confusion. They would paw at the wounded cow, but would not run to protect themselves. Their hearing was so poor, and their eyesight, too, that they would never know that they were being shot so long as the buffalo runner stayed up here on this hill, about two hundred and fifty yards away from the herd.

The big Sharps rifle would drop each of them, one shot one kill, after that. The buffalo runners had to be good shots. At three dollars a hide, a buffalo runner could not afford the powder and lead if it took more than one shot to drop a bison.

Once the herd was all shot dead – twenty to thirty to a herd, usually – then the skinners would go to work. They cut off the hide and cut out the tongue. Maybe, if they needed some jerky, they would strip some meat from the shoulders of a couple of the bison. But mostly they just left the meat for the buzzards. In a few months, someone would come along and gather up the bones for the bone mill.

Usually, the buffalo runners would leave the skinners to their work and go off to find another herd, but they had camped here and made jerky, and that was a couple of days of work. Minko was confident that he was close now to this group of buffalo runners.

Minko rode around the campsite until he saw the tracks of the wagons where the runners had departed. He knew the tracks would take him down to the killing ground where the buffalo carcass rotted and stank. He would follow the tracks quickly from there so as not to linger among the stench longer than necessary.

He knew from the tracks, but also from the

information he had gathered in Gainesville, that he was following two wagons, at least a couple of horses, the mule teams and some spare mules. There were two shooters among this group and at least half a dozen skinners. Some folks in Gainesville had said there were eight skinners, others said they'd seen them leave out with six.

Minko hoped to catch up to the buffalo runners today. It was still morning, plenty of daylight left. His horse was fresh, and other than the heat, he felt pretty good. It would be a good day to make a fast ride. The grass was tall, and the wagons made easy tracks to follow.

Minko held warrants for two skinners who were claimed to be in this buffalo runner's team. Wes Simpson and a Mexican by the name of Cortez. The men were wanted on charges of defrauding the federal government by selling stolen cattle at Fort Richardson.

The buffalo runners got their start from Gainesville and had left out of there a week ahead of Minko. He'd wanted to take them in the town but had missed them by a week. He hoped to catch up to them today and get back to the sheriff's office at Gainesville as soon as possible. He was eager to be home, back in Two Rivers Station.

He didn't expect much trouble from Simpson and Cortez. Neither of them had any known background of violence. They were just a couple of cow punchers and buff skinners who'd seen an opportunity to rustle some cattle and make some easy money. They'd pay a small price for their crime. The federal judge, Fitzsimmons, would likely fine them restitution to pay back the government and let them off with whatever time they stayed in the sheriff's jail. The biggest trouble would likely come from the buffalo runner, the man pulling the trigger on the big Sharps rifle.

The only way for buffalo runners to make money was to shoot and skin a mess of buffalo as fast as possible. Losing two of his skinners would be troublesome to him. And if he had no skinners other than Simpson and Cortez, the man might be as inclined to shoot Minko as to let his skinners go.

The other thing was Comanche. No man liked riding the plains, and especially not alone, and that included those who bluffed big and brave. In his heart, every man on the range – gunslinger, outlaw, lawman, buffalo runner, cow puncher – feared a Comanche attack above all else.

The Comanche never attacked when the numbers were even. They always overwhelmed their enemies. They employed surprise and speed in their attacks, and often they trailed their enemies for many miles, observing before striking. And if the Comanche caught you alive, God have mercy on you.

Minko's black horse was a good mount. He'd run all day and night. If it came to an Indian attack, Minko was certain he could outrun them. But if they took him unawares, in his sleep or down in a creek bed getting water – he shuddered to think about it.

The bravest of men held fear in their heart over a Comanche raid.

The soldiers were out in force, though. The cavalry was patrolling all through the plains, and Minko was not more than fifty or sixty miles from a couple of army camps and a fort. Minko trusted the proximity of the cavalry to keep the Comanche away.

Not more than five miles from the last camp, Minko rode up on a second buffalo kill. Two dozen of the dead beasts were rotting here, and judging from the smell they had spent about the same amount of time in the summer sun as the last bunch. The nearness of the two kills told Minko that the buffalo runner had probably killed the first batch in the morning and this batch in the afternoon. The skinners would have spent all morning on the first buffalo herd and they'd have spent the afternoon on this one. That was probably two days prior. Minko believed he was nearing his prey.

The wagon tracks came near to a stream now, a tiny creek that would have provided water to the mules and horses and the men. It was probably late afternoon when they got moving, and they followed the creek so they would be near to it when they decided to camp. When Minko reached the camp, he would be a day behind Simpson and Cortez, and just now the sun was directly overhead. He might still reach them before sunset.

***

The creek he was following had occasional cottonwoods growing on its banks, but like many streams on the plains it was largely unmarked by vegetation, and from two hundred yards off you might not even know it was there. Creeks on the plains weren't usually more than just a narrow and shallow cut across the landscape. Minko often wondered about men crossing the deserts and plains in the old days, before the white men came, and he was curious if men in those days ever died of thirst with a creek not a mile away. Of course, there were probably a couple of months in the year, July and August, maybe, when the creek ran dry and would offer no succor to man nor beast.

Off in the distance now, Minko could see what looked like a lone cottonwood, and his interest in it was only to mark the passage of distance. He'd been marking time by some very distant hills, but they were so far off that they grew too slow and made him feel like he wasn't getting very far. But the cottonwood grew more quickly, and then it started to take shape, and Minko realized it was no cottonwood after all, but a covered wagon. He expected he was about to come upon his quarry.

Minko drew the Henry rifle from its scabbard and held it across his lap as he neared the wagon, but he soon came to believe there was something amiss.

The canvas covering of the wagon was torn and blowing in the hot breeze.

There was neither beast nor man moving around by the wagon. No mules nor horses were staked near the wagon.

As he approached, Minko understood what had happened. The Comanche had attacked.

Below the wagon, Minko could see the body of a man who'd sought shelter there. And beyond the wagon, another man's body lay in the tall grass.

Minko urged his horse forward, his eyes straining across the grassland for any sign of the Comanche who'd struck against the buffalo runners.

The men had camped here. There was a burned out campfire. The wagon that remained in the camp had been the supply wagon, and the supplies were looted all out of it. The looting occurred without care – gunpowder was spilled, a sack of flour and a bag of salt were both left. Clean clothes and tools had been tossed onto the ground.

The man in the grass nearest the wagon was shot through many times. The Comanche seldom had good guns. Those men who traded with the Comanche were as frightened and distrustful of the Comanche as any other man, and when they traded guns to the Comanche they typically traded poor guns. The Comanche only got good guns through raids. These Comanche were using good guns. They had shot accurately. The wagon was scarred with many shots that came near to man who was under the wagon.

The shot that got him had hit him in the side. From the blood smeared in the grass below the wagon, Minko believed this man had suffered for some time, slowly bleeding to death.

The scene presented puzzles that Minko struggled to solve.

The two bodies Minko could readily see had been left undisturbed. Some said the Comanche did not take a scalp from a dead man. Minko assumed this was true, though he did not know it to be so. But that would explain the man in the grass. His scalp was intact because he was killed quickly by the bullets that struck his body. But the man under the wagon was alive when the Comanche looted the wagon. Yet he also still had his scalp. The Comanche seldom missed an opportunity to torture a victim with knives and fire. It made no sense to Minko that they would have left this man to bleed out.

The Comanche took the mules and the horses, and that made sense. But he did not know the Comanche to take a wagon and buffalo pelts. A raiding party would not want to be encumbered by a wagon. And if they would take one, why not take two? And the supplies that were looted – in what way did the Comanche transport those supplies? The buffalo runners had harvested enough buffalo skins that there would not be room in the one wagon for all the supplies as well.

Down in the creek bank Minko found two more bodies, and these two fit the descriptions of Cortez and Simpson. Minko's mission into the plains was for naught, now. There was nothing the Yankee judge could do to Simpson and Cortez now that the Comanche had not already done.

Again, though, they were shot and had died of their wounds and their bodies were left undisturbed.

Away from the wagon and the creek, Minko found another victim. This was one of the two shooters with this band of buffalo runners. His Sharps rifle was beside his body. The Comanche would have considered that Sharps rifle to be a real prize, but the gun had been struck by a lead ball and the forestock was splintered and the barrel dented.

The man had defended himself and his camp in the same way he shot buffalo. His gun stand was also there with his body. He had fought admirably, though. Minko counted six bullet wounds. He'd been shot in the thigh, the hip, the gut, and the shoulder. A bullet had skimmed the side of his head and opened up a gash. But the shot in his chest had ended his life. Perhaps he was still working the Sharps even though it was damaged. The gut wound probably would have been a mortal wound, but it wasn't going to kill him outright.

This was a hard man who'd lived a rough life. He bore the look of it on his white-whiskered face. An examination of the body, Minko suspected, would reveal plenty more wounds, too. Minko did not know, but he guessed this was a man who came to the frontier in the '40s. Maybe fought the Mexicans. Maybe fought the Yankees. Definitely this was not his first encounter with the

Comanche. Minko guessed that so many lead balls and pointed tip arrows had been sent in this man's direction that sooner or later one of them was likely to put an end to him.

Minko did not spend more time examining the body. Like the others, the old timer had kept his hair.

Too much of this was a puzzle, but Minko believed he could find the solution.

He stepped back into the saddle and rode through the tall grass looking for the thread of a clue on which he could give a tug and allow the mystery to begin to unravel.

The dead men had been facing east. The attack had come from that direction, forcing them to have their backs to the creek. Though not deep, the creek bank would have prevented the men from making an escape without abandoning their wagons.

Minko searched for the thread he was seeking in that direction, looking out across the tall grass. There were low hills to the east and the southeast. These hills could hide a band of Comanche and could serve as a vantage point from which to make an attack, except that they were a good three hundred yards away. Minko did not know many Comanche who could make accurate shots from three hundred yards.

But then he saw the loose thread.

It was a faint trail in the grass, left by the wheels of a wagon that had come from the hills in the east. The grass was bent to the west. Someone had brought a wagon from point of the ambush down to the buffalo runners' camp. Minko did not know Comanche raiding parties to use wagons.

But the loose thread was beginning to unravel the mystery.

If it was white men, and not Comanche, who attacked the buffalo runners, then perhaps they used big Sharps or Remington rifles. Practiced men could make that shot from the hills. It would explain why they did not take both wagons. The white men loaded the looted supplies into their own wagon and took the animals, and they also stole the wagon with the buffalo skins.

Now the scene began to make more sense.

He had discovered the bodies of five men and believed there must be at least one more. But the man might have run in any direction. He might have crossed the creek and fled west when the other men in his outfit were killed. He might have fled on horseback or he might have run on foot. For that matter, the man might be lying dead in the tall grass in any direction. The grass was tall enough that a body might difficult to discover even if Minko rode right past it.

Minko wondered over the technicalities of jurisdiction in this case. The men he sought were dead. Murders on the open range in Texas were a gray area. In the coming months Texas was expected to be allowed back in the Union, and then very clearly he would have no jurisdiction. But now, with Texas official a territory under the control of the federal government, Minko's role as a deputy U.S. Marshal was extensive.

The Chickasaw lawman easily found the wagon trail that departed south, and studying the tracks he could see that they belonged to two wagons. The men had driven single file to hide this, but wheels of the wagon with the buffalo pelts were wider, and the narrow wheels of the other wagon were visible.

Minko followed the tracks for a ways, perhaps a mile, when he heard a shot from somewhere south of him. It was distant and not particularly loud, but it was unquestionably someone firing a single shot.

Staying on the tracks of the wagons, Minko urged his horse forward. Whether it was his jurisdiction or not, he intended to continue pulling the thread.

***

Minko staked the black horse down at the base of a small hill and crouched as he ran up to the top of it. He'd heard a second shot, and this one was close. He believed from the top of the hill he would be able to gain a vantage point.

He had his hand wrapped around the brass receiver of the Henry so that the gun would make no gleam in the late afternoon sun.

At the top of the hill he kneeled down into the tall grass and removed his hat. Now he watched.

In the distance he could see the wagons and the animals – several mules and horses. One was a good covered, the second was loaded with buffalo skins.

Minko had seen buff runners come into town before, and he knew that the buffalo runners did not come in until the skins were stacked eight or ten feet high. This one was not stacked more than five feet high.

There were a half dozen men around the wagons, all of them hunkered down behind the wagons. They were looking south, away from Minko, and they were fully exposed to the deputy marshal.

On a hill beyond the wagons, farther to the south, Minko thought he could see a small dark spot that might be a man, a black mass hidden among the tall grass.

One of the men down at the wagons was using the back corner of the wagon to steady his Sharps rifle. He was aiming it at the dark spot on top of the hill.

The men at the wagons had ambushed the buffalo runners. One of them had gotten away, fled to the south, and was now ambushing the ambushers.

But why?

Were personal grudges being settled on the range? Did the ambushers simply want a wagonload of buffalo pelts? It seemed like a poor reason for murder, but life on the range was never worth much except to the man who owned it.

Minko was not more than a hundred yards from the wagons. The man on the hilltop was another hundred and fifty yards beyond them. The men at the wagons were easy range for the Henry rifle, and Minko was fairly certain he could hit the man on the hilltop, but probably not before the man on the hilltop could get him with the Sharps.

The man at the corner of the wagon let loose a shot with his rifle. Minko watched to see if there was any sign that the man on the hilltop was hit. He did not think so. The black spot was still there. The man with the rifle at the wagon was reloading.

Minko counted four men among the wagons, but with closer inspection he saw that one of the men was kneeling next to a body. That was probably the work of the first shot Minko heard.

He might intervene. He had the drop on the men at the wagons, and they were pinned down. A shot in among them might be enough to convince them to throw down their guns. It might not, though. And Minko wondered if the man on the hilltop would be satisfied turning these men over to a U.S. Marshal. Or would that man only be satisfied with trading blood for blood?

The man at the wagon took another shot. Minko was fairly certain this one told. The black mass on the far hill jumped. Minko watched to see if the man would slump to the ground, but even as he watched, Minko saw a puff of smoke rise from the mass. The corner of the wagon splintered, and the man standing there dropped his rifle and stumbled backwards. Minko watched, believing at first that the shooter at the wagon had been hit, but it was the gun, not the man, that was hit. The man was examining the rifle now.

Minko was not watching when the second shot was fired. The man on the hill had two rifles. Minko heard it and watched as one of the men down by the wagons grabbed at his stomach. Gut shot. That man would die before he came off this plain.

"I'm shot!" the man hollered. He writhed for a bit on the ground. None of the other men in his outfit came to his assistance. They all held their protected positions.

Minko could see movement on the hill. The shooter with the two Sharps rifles was reloading.

Minko felt the tension in his stomach. He was glad he wasn't down there among those men by the wagons. The man on the hill with the Sharps rifles could hit a buffalo with a kill shot in the neck from three hundred yards. The men by the wagons were waiting to die, and they had to

119

know that.

The man who'd been gut shot was talking, but Minko could not hear him. Probably asking for water. That had to make it worse for those not yet shot.

The buffalo runner was good at his work. Minko saw another man fall just as he heard the shot, and this man was dead when he hit the ground. The buffalo runner with the two Sharps rifles was killing men the same way he killed buffalo.

Only two men were left at the wagons. One of them broke from his cover and ran to a horse that had wandered away from the wagons to graze in the grass, oblivious to the murder taking place behind him. The man grabbed the horse's reins and stepped into the stirrup. Minko was not surprised when he heard the report of the rifle from across the way and saw the man stretch out and then slump down over the horse's back. The horse bolted and run, and the shot man fell from the back of the horse.

The last man at the wagons was the one who had tried to return fire and had his gun shot from his hand. He was the smarter man. He knew the man on the hill now had to reload and there was time. The man down at the wagon broke into a run now, he grabbed a horse and threw himself into the saddle. He wheeled the horse back north and gave it spurs. The horse broke into a gallop.

Minko scurried back down the hill to his black Morgan and stepped quickly into the saddle. He kept the Henry in his hand and urged his horse forward. He intended to intercept the rider as he came out from behind the hill.

With the Henry rifle in one hand and the reins in the other, Minko urged the black horse alongside the fleeing man.

"Whoa there!" Minko called. "I'm a Deputy United States Marshal! Rein in that horse, now!"

He heard the report of the rifle, and the man's horse collapsed in a flurry of dust and legs. The man was thrown well wide, but he was obviously hurt from the fall.

"You shot?" Minko said.

The man pushed himself from the ground with one arm. The other hung limp, broken from the fall. He started stumbling away, but Minko rode the Morgan into the man and knocked him down. Now Minko leapt from his saddle and put his knee into the man's back to hold him down. Minko slid the man's six shooter out of its holster and flung it toward the creek.

"I told you I'm a Deputy United States Marshal," Minko repeated. "I'm arresting you for ambushing them buffalo runners back there."

"I'm the one who was ambushed!" the man yelled. "You saw it – he just shot my horse!"

"Hush up, now," Minko said. "That man's liable to shoot us again. Now don't you move."

Minko took from his saddle bag one of the two sets of wrist irons he'd brought with him, intended for Simpson and Cortez.

"I seen what you done," Minko said. "Y'all ambushed them buffalo runners, and you didn't know there was another one out here. He paid you back in turn."

The man did not bother arguing.

Minko hoped the buffalo hunter with the two rifles would hold his fire. To be safe, though, he stood behind his black Morgan and waited.

After a time, Minko saw the man walking down from the hill where he'd made his stand. Both rifles were in his hands down at his side. The man made his way toward the horses and wagons first. Minko watched him put the Sharps rifles down in one of the wagons and get a revolver from the holster of one of the men he'd shot.

The man continued his walk toward Minko.

"I 'preciate you stopping this man for me," the buffalo runner said.

"I'm a Deputy U.S. Marshal," Minko said, and he slid his duster away so that the badge on his vest was visible. "I'm taking this man in for murdering the men in your outfit back there."

"Ain't no need," the buffalo runner said. "I can see to him."

"Naw," Minko said. "You saw to the others. This one comes with me. I'll be obliged if you turn over one of them horses so I can ride him back to the sheriff in Gainesville. But the rest of it, the wagon and the mules and the other horses, you can take all the rest."

"I can't drive two wagons. And I've still got my other wagon a few miles north of here where they left it."

Minko spat into the dirt.

"Well, seeing as how my prisoner here put you to all this trouble, we'll let him drive the wagon with the pelts. That away, you get something out of his being alive, and I still get to bring my prisoner in without having to fight you over him."

***

Minko did not stay in Gainesville long enough to see the hanging. He'd seen plenty of men killed, and reckoned he'd see plenty more, and a hanging didn't hold any interest to him. The sheriff didn't mind sharing his opinion that Minko should have let the buffalo runner kill the man.

The buffalo runner found some folks who were willing to ride out onto the prairie with him for the dual purpose of fetching his wagon and burying the men who'd been in his outfit.

Minko didn't think it mattered enough to tell anyone that he'd been out there to bring Cortez and Simpson in on federal warrants. It was not lost on Minko that if he'd caught them in Gainesville before they left to hunt buffalo, they'd still be alive. But any man who lived on the frontier knew that time was a precise thing. The sun rose at sunup and it set at sundown. And when a man's time was at its end, time had a way of finding him wherever he was.

THANK YOU!

Thank you so much for reading
The Yankee Star!

If you enjoyed the book, please consider leaving a review. I really appreciate feedback from readers, and it helps me to know how to focus future writing efforts when readers let me know what I got right (or even where I missed the mark) with my stories.

If you enjoyed this Two Rivers Station Western, I would encourage you to check out some of the other Western and Frontier Adventure novels I have written, and periodically check my website (robertpeecher.com) for updates.

The Two Rivers Station Westerns is an ongoing series, and Jack and Honor, Zeke and Minko, Jason and even Ma White are sure to be back again. We'd love for you to join us where the two rivers meet with each new novel!

If you have not yet, please sign up for my newsletter at robertpeecher.com and follow my Facebook page "Robert Peecher Novels," and you can be among the first to know when I have new releases.

ABOUT THE AUTHOR

When he's not living in the 1800s through his Western and
Civil War fiction, Robert Peecher is often found paddling
rivers, hiking trails, sending lead down range, spending time
with his three sons, or hanging out with his first reader, best
friend, and wife Jean.

OTHER NOVELS BY ROBERT PEECHER

THE LODERO WESTERNS: Lodero is a gunslinger bent on
keeping a graveside promise to his mother: To find out what
happened to his father who set off to seek a fortune and all
that ever came home was an empty trunk.

ANIMAS FORKS: Animas Forks, Colorado, is the largest city
in America (at 14,000 feet). The town has everything you could
want in a Frontier Boomtown: cutthroats, ne'er-do-wells,
whores, backshooters, drunks, thieves, and murderers. And
there's also some unsavory folks who show up.

JACKSON SPEED: Scoundrels are not born, they are made.
The Jackson Speed series follows the life of a true coward
making his way through 1800s America – from the Mexican
American War through the Civil War and into the Old West.
"The history is true and the fiction is fun!"

FIND THESE AND OTHER NOVELS BY
ROBERT PEECHER AT AMAZON.COM